THE IMPOSTOR

Modern Scandinavian
Literature in Translation
MSLT

Editor: Robert E. Bjork,
Arizona State University

Board Members:
Evelyn Firchow,
University of Minnesota
Niels Ingwersen,
University of Wisconsin
Torborg Lundell,
University of California,
Santa Barbara
Patricia McFate,
Past President,
The American-Scandinavian
Foundation
Harald S. Naess,
University of Wisconsin
Sven H. Rossel,
University of Washington
Paul Schach,
University of Nebraska–
Lincoln
George C. Schoolfield,
Yale University
Ross Shideler,
University of California,
Los Angeles

Fugls Føde by Peter Seeberg

THE
IMPOSTOR

Translated
by Anni Whissen

Afterword
by Niels Ingwersen

University
of Nebraska Press

Lincoln &
London : 1990

Originally published in
        Denmark by Arena as *Fugls Føde*,
        © by Peter Seeberg 1957
Translation and afterword copy-
        right © 1990 by the
        University of Nebraska Press
        All rights reserved
        Manufactured in the United
        States of America
The paper in this book meets the mini-
        mum requirements of
        American National Standard for
        Information Sciences –
        Permanence of Paper
        for Printed Library Materials,
        ANSI Z39.48-1984.
Library of Congress
        Cataloging in Publication Data
        Seeberg, Peter.
        [Fugls føde. English] The impostor
        (Fugls føde) /
        by Peter Seeberg ; translated by
        Anni Whissen ;
        afterword by Niels Ingwersen.
        p.   cm. – (Modern
        Scandinavian literature in trans-
        lation) Translation of:
        Fugls føde. ISBN 0-8032-4190-9
        ISBN 0-8032-9201-5
        I. Title.   II. Series.
        PT8175.S4415F813   1990
        839.8'1374 – dc20   89-29960   CIP

PT
8175
.S4415
F813
1990

To Hanne

328069

Contents

THE IMPOSTOR

1.

A chair scraped. Maybe someone was coming. He jumped up and hurried into the other room, where she was standing by the window looking out. He squeezed in next to her and put his arm around her soft waist, hoping to placate her. She had stayed in bed that morning, and they had not had a chance to talk yet.

'Is anyone coming, dear?' Tom said ingratiatingly and managed to push his head forward so he could see out.

'How should I know,' she snapped. Out on the road a boy of about ten stood and stared at the house. When he saw the two grown-ups standing close to the window, he lost courage and moved away a few steps with his head lowered until the hedge concealed him. But a little while later he appeared again with a forlorn look on his face. He disappeared a second time, but suddenly he came running all out of breath, gingerly making his way across the narrow boards that had been laid across the mud oozing from around the leaky pump hose, and a moment later he was hammering on the door.

Tom went to the door and opened it.

'Phone for you at the grocer's,' the boy yelled.

It was not the grocer's own delivery boy, Tom noticed.

The boy was already hurrying back over the narrow bridges, past the pump motor and the excavation, which was full of water with a bit of foundation jutting up here and there. Tom turned to Etna.

'I've got a phone call. I'd better run up to the grocer's. I'll bet you they've accepted one of my things.'

1

'Accepted?' she snapped.

'Want anything while I'm there?' Tom called while running around looking for his coat. 'What do we need? Couldn't we use a can of Portuguese sardines for lunch? And what about kerosene for the stove?'

'But you don't have any money,' Etna said in a flat voice.

'They'll just have to put it on the bill,' Tom shouted. 'I'll get us some lemon, too. I'll bet it's about my latest story.'

'More likely, it's the lawyer,' Etna said and sat down.

'When I'm done, we're going to take a trip, honey,' Tom said, putting one foot up on a chair to tie his shoelace.

'You haven't written one line yet,' she said.

'I have too,' he insisted.

'And just when was that, if I may ask?'

'To Italy,' he continued his train of thought.

When he got to the door, she looked up from her magazine.

'You come back again, you hear?' There was suddenly something urgent, dangerous in her voice.

'Of course, dear. Now, if it's your sister, is there any message? Think you'd like to go see her today? I bet it would do you good.'

Tom slipped out the door. Balancing from board to board in the mud, he stumbled and got the tip of his shoe wet in the slush, but he could wipe it off before he got to the grocer's. He would have to lay some more boards down. There were some in the neighbor's yard, and it couldn't do any harm to borrow a couple until there was a hard frost or the water had soaked into the ground.

He hurried down the poorly paved road, his collar up over his ears. The weather was miserable, as it had been all this fall. Rain and more rain. The summer, too, had been rainy and cold. They had been forced to sit inside and mope most of the time. Today it was sea fog that went right through you and that severed the last leaves from the skeletons of the trees. There would probably be a frost soon, and the day would come when they would have to give up and move in with their families until spring came and they were beginning to think they couldn't do without each other, and they would move out to the house again and live these days that were so inevitable.

He was in a hurry as he always was when he walked by himself. It was in him to push forward, even though he was just as likely to turn back. He saw nothing around him as he walked. Other people would stop at the edge of the sidewalk and watch him hurry by, and children digging with little shovels in the gravel heaps hesitated for a moment, knowing instinctively that something had to be up if anyone was in that much of a hurry.

As he crossed the gravel in front of the grocery store, he was hailed by Bergstrøm, the grocer, who was pumping gas.

'Someone just called and asked for you.'

Tom continued his way toward the stairs and took them in three bounds. In the doorway he turned around and answered, 'It's probably from a magazine.'

'More likely it's someone who wants money,' Bergstrøm grinned, turning toward the driver.

Mrs. Bergstrøm was weighing sugar.

'Hello, Mrs. Bergstrøm,' Tom said. 'I'm sorry to be such a bother about the phone.'

'It does happen rather frequently,' she said, putting her index finger on the scales. 'Aren't you going to finish that house of yours someday soon? Really, you can't go on living the way you do.'

'Guess so,' Tom mumbled.

'It's a good thing you don't have any children,' the wife said. 'Children ought to have a real home. You can thank your lucky stars you don't have any. The phone is in there if that's what you're waiting for.'

'Thanks,' Tom said and raced into the office.

'The telephone was on the desk between heaps of invoices, but he couldn't miss the note. Tom found it right away. He read the number but didn't recognize it. While trying to guess who it might be, he caught sight of carton upon carton of cigarettes stacked on nearby shelves along the wall. He fished a pack out of an open carton and put it in his pocket. Then he bent over and dialed the operator.

It took a while. He paced back and forth for a while with the receiver to his ear and then grabbed another pack of cigarettes. Glancing back over his shoulder, he was just about to slip it into his pocket when Mrs. Bergstrøm's eyes met his. Then he raised the pack in the air, waving it at her and smiling. At that moment the operator came on the line, and he asked for the number while trying to tear open the pack with one hand. He finally managed to fish out a cigarette and stood there playing with it in his hand.

The telephone rang. Tom put the cigarette in his mouth and sat down on top of the invoices with his legs up on the desk chair. He kept an eye on Mrs. Bergstrøm, who was in the process of arranging the paper money in neat stacks in the cash register.

'Hello,' someone said.

'Hello there,' Tom said, putting his cigarette behind his ear. 'You called. What can I do for you?'

'Is that you, Tom?' the voice said. 'It's really great I got hold of you. So you got out of the big city?'

'Hiffs, right?' Tom said. 'Sure, a man's got to get out in the country and have a little peace, you know, so I'm building a house out here and all.'

'How about that,' Hiffs said laughing. 'Wouldn't have thought you'd try that sort of thing.'

'Sure, why not?' Tom said. 'At least, that way the landlord can't throw you out. And if you want to write, you've got more peace and quiet. After all, there's no noise out here.'

'Keeping busy then?' Hiffs said.

'No, not really,' Tom said. 'You know how it is. You're your own boss. You do a lot of thinking and reminiscing and try to make something of it. I'm writing a novel, you know, and that's a bit harder than writing out invoices. You have to get started somehow.'

'Any chance you could come into town?' Hiffs said.

'Just where are you? Sounds tempting.'

'How about meeting me on the old pedestrian bridge,' Hiffs said.

'Fine with me.'

'So it's a date?'

'Sure, any special time?'

'I'll be in the area, so I'll be watching for you. And hey, try to get here as soon as you can,' Hiffs said with a quiet laugh.

'I'll be there,' Tom said.

'Good,' Hiffs said. 'See you.'

'Bye,' Tom said. He heard Hiffs hang up, but he still shouted, 'Say, have you got any money?'

It was too late. He waited a moment, then put the phone down and stuck the cigarette into the corner of his mouth. He went out into the shop.

'Thanks for letting me use your phone, Mrs. Bergstrøm,' he said. 'Could you let me have a box of matches and then put it on the bill with the cigarettes?'

'It really isn't customary here for people to help themselves,' Mrs. Bergstrøm said.

Tom scrutinized the shelves.

'Say, Mrs. Bergstrøm, would you happen to have some of those Portuguese sardines called "Nice"?'

'Do you have any idea how much you owe?'

'Ah, but now I'm getting money, Mrs. Bergstrøm. You'll have the whole amount by Saturday. Let me see what kind of sardines you've got.'

Mrs. Bergstrøm got out three or four cans and put them down with a bang one by one right in front of him.

'You haven't got any "Nice" sardines?'

'Just listen to him, "neese" this and "neese" that. Of course, we eat the Danish ones ourselves. They're cheaper!'

Tom paid no attention to anything she said.

'Let me have that can.' He put it in his pocket and made for the door. Bergstrøm was on his way up the stairs. Tom hurried out, moved aside, and took off down the road.

Bergstrøm looked after him through the store window.

'Did you give him anything?' he said.

'He helped himself,' the wife said.

'Might as well forget about that money . . .'

'You've got to tell him next time he comes that he can't get anything else here until he has paid up,' the wife said.

'Yeah, things have gone far enough,' Bergstrøm said seriously. 'Shouldn't we be sending him a letter?'

'No, you'll have to have a talk with him.'

'Okay, I'll see what I can do about it.'

Tom almost ran back to the house. He had no idea what it was Hiffs wanted of him, but he was sure there was something behind it. He could only guess at what that might be, but whatever it was, he figured something good, maybe even profitable, was bound to come of it; but the encouraging thing about it was the exhilarating feeling of being set in motion by somebody else who asked him to come and of suddenly being liberated from his own existence so that he could let himself drift weightlessly through the redeeming spheres of other people's decisions.

Hiffs was a strange fellow. Tom couldn't come up with any other term for the erratic intensity of his talents. He always had something cooking, original projects that he started, ran with, and then abandoned because they bored him or because he didn't want to get stuck. Money found its way into his pockets just as readily as into a bank, but he acted as if he didn't notice. That's the kind of guy you should latch on to. He would drop generous crumbs from his table, but Hiffs had never let Tom get anywhere, although Tom had been ready to transform himself into whatever it took for his sake. Hiffs had kept him at a distance and had never accepted one single offer of his services.

It was strange that he should call now, but Hiffs would always be Hiffs. He probably had use for him — he had used others before. They came and went, women of all kinds and men from all walks of life and with various points of view, and they always seemed to fulfill his wishes satisfactorily, but either he never kept them, or they didn't keep him. He would disappear for a while and then pop up in new circles. But what did Hiffs want with him? He knew him only from chance meetings now and then, but there must have been some point to this series of coincidences, Tom thought, because now it seemed that Hiffs could finally use him.

Tom paid no attention to the mud splashing in his face as he ran across the boards in front of the house. He pushed the door open, took one long step into the room, and said, 'Now we'll get money. We can finish the house. It was one of my old buddies that called. He's got loads of money – in fact, money is no big deal to him.'

Etna looked up from her magazine.

'Aren't you a mess! How is it you always manage to get yourself so dirty? And just look at your face! What a sight you are!'

'And you know what?' Tom said. 'I got Mrs. Bergstrøm to let me have a can of sardines. You're welcome to have them for lunch. I've got to leave right away. You won't feel bad about that, will you? I also got cigarettes. You can have half the pack. That'll be something to keep you company, okay?'

'Thanks a lot. It's really great being stuck here all day.'

'When we get the house finished and the garden laid out, things will be much better, honey. I'm sure Hiffs has got something up his sleeve. I can just feel it.'

'And what have you got to offer?'

'That's not important. He's happy as long as you can help him shape an idea. The rest takes care of itself. It's nothing that takes any special talent, just good ideas, and those I've got plenty of.'

'You haven't even written one line of your book.'

'It's hard to get started, you know. It's a matter of finding the right words, Etna. You know how it is.'

'You've been sitting there staring out the window for eons. I can't go on like this. Here I sit, and here you sit, and nothing

7

ever happens, and you find any old excuse to take off every time you get the chance, and I wait and wait for you, and you don't come home, and when you do, you never bring anything with you.'

'Sure I do, Etna. I just now brought you a can of sardines.'

'I don't even like sardines.'

'Fine, I'll run up and exchange them.'

'You never do anything for me, not a thing. You just sit there and stare, and when I talk to you, you don't bother to answer.'

'I know, Etna, but now things will get better.'

Etna burst out laughing, but she stopped abruptly with a stifled 'You – you – you?'

When she had pulled herself together, her eyes filled with tears, but she stammered, 'You are a real nitwit.'

Now she's okay, Tom thought.

'But Etna,' he said, 'Etna . . .'

'Go wash your face,' she said.

He got out his handkerchief and spat on a corner of it.

'You pig,' she said. 'Are you going to rub spit all over your face? What a terrific guy I married. I was really stupid. What a mistake I made.'

Tom poured a little water into the basin and rinsed his face.

'You don't think I could have anybody else?' Etna said.

'Sure,' Tom said, 'but no one would love you as much as I do. You know that, Etna.'

'A lot of good it does,' she said, starting to sob, 'when I can't even tell.'

'No, Etna, I agree. That's my big failing,' Tom said, 'but I've got to run now, honey. Take care. Things will work out. I'm sure there's money in Hiffs.'

When Etna looked up, Tom was already down the three steps and on his way out toward the road.

She jumped up and opened the door.

'Do you have a clean handkerchief?' she said in a voice hoarse from crying. Tom turned around and pulled a large blue handkerchief out of his coat pocket, waving it as he continued to walk backwards.

'Here, look,' he yelled. 'It's almost clean.'

'All right,' she said in despair.

Tom waved to her with wild gestures, and she slowly pulled the door shut and plopped down into the wicker chair.

Tom walked down the path leading toward the main road and the square where the bus to the city stopped. The neighbor's dog followed him for a while and jumped up at him a couple of times, but he didn't notice; however, his instinct told him to cross the street and look away as he passed the butcher's shop, because the butcher had come out and called after him several times before when he had walked by.

At the bus stop a dozen women with small children were already waiting in line. Tom positioned himself several feet away and turned the pockets of his coat, jacket, and pants inside out without finding anything. He got impatient and walked back and forth along the edge of the sidewalk without knowing what to do. He continued his pacing until the bus stopped and the doors opened. Then he piously joined the line, which was being admitted in small groups.

'Downtown,' Tom said and alternately put his hands in his left and right pockets. 'You'll have to take my name down. I forgot my money. Well, I guess that won't matter, will it?'

The bus driver shook his head knowingly.

'Okay,' Tom said and got off again. He made his way across the sidewalk and went into a tobacco shop, where he leaned with his hands on the counter and rocked back and forth in this position until the trim, balding tobacconist came through the door to the back room.

'May I help you?' he said.

'Listen,' Tom said, 'I wonder if you would be kind enough to help me out of a bind. I left my billfold at home, you see, and I've got to catch a bus downtown. Do you think you could let me exchange a pack of cigarettes for a couple of kroner? I've got the cigarettes right here, there's nothing wrong with them, I guarantee it, but if you'd just let me have a couple of kroner, you'd be doing me a big favor. I think I'd just have time enough to catch the bus, it usually waits here for the one coming from town.'

'I'd be very happy to give you the full amount,' the tobacconist said calmly. 'It could happen to anyone.'

'That's for sure,' Tom said. 'This is really nice of you. Thanks a lot.'

He dashed out the door. The door to the bus had been shut, but Tom banged on it till the driver let him in.

'Well, I hit it lucky,' Tom said, chuckling a couple of times. 'One ticket to town.'

'No need to beat on the door like that, buddy,' the bus driver said. 'You'll ruin the finish. You might have waited till I opened up. There you go!'

The bus started off with a jerk. Tom weaved down the middle aisle and finally lurched onto a one-seater in the back of the bus.

2.

The bus sped through the city dump areas toward the inner suburbs. Tom lay halfway down in his seat, trying to suppress the nausea he felt from the bumps and the diesel fumes. Whenever the bus made a turn, his stomach heaved, but he kept hoping it would get better when they reached the brand-new paved road that was smooth and straight as a ribbon. He craned his neck a little, looking over his seat at the other passengers, who were sitting upright as they stared at the city's cardboard skyline. He seemed to be the only one suffering from the ride, maybe because he hadn't had anything to eat. He struggled with his coat, trying to get into the pockets of his jacket where he might find something to smoke. When he had lit a bent cigarette, he began to feel good again.

He was chock-full of ideas. He felt them crammed together in his brain, simply waiting for instructions to be given. Then he would be right there, because if there was one thing he knew for sure, it was that he was the type of person who had ideas. As a matter of fact, Tom might very well have exactly what Hiffs was looking for.

They had reached the new road. The vibrations in the chassis ceased, but the rear end was still pitching. Tom looked out the rear window where the view of the refuse desert was compressed into narrow slots between the one-story houses lining the suburban street. That was more or less the kind of house he was building, though of course it wouldn't be as manicured, as neat in a bourgeois sort of way, but he got shivers down his spine at the thought that he might actually someday succeed in resuming work on his novel, that he might, in fact, complete it.

He sank back in his seat. The driver started to apply the brakes following a nasty curve, and the contents of his stomach rose to a dangerous level and then receded. As the bus started up again, it was as if a magnet were sucking the whole mess upwards, upwards, while a sweet pain circled his brain. Tom cursed the driver to the deepest hellhole.

Hiffs probably wanted some kind of advertising, a good idea made into a clever little brochure or a slogan that could be placed where no one would miss it. He could take care of that, all right. He wasn't particular. It occurred to Tom that he had written the battle song for the communist party's fourth district. It was his neighbor, a sewer worker, who had begged him to do it, for naturally it had to bear his name, and he had received ten kroner for it. It hadn't taken him ten minutes to write.

'We are the sons of work'

it began. Good Lord, why not give those poor slobs something to believe in and to live for. He wouldn't even mind establishing himself as a writer of battle songs if someone would just pay him ten kroner per song. Gradually, of course, he would charge more. The conservatives ought to pay at least two hundred. He got a kick out of thinking about how absolutely indifferent he felt about prostituting himself or selling out or whatever else they might call it. No, he wasn't particular.

That was why he wouldn't mind selling himself lock, stock, and barrel to Hiffs, if only there were money in it. It was a lot more comfortable than playing the buffoon for the party hacks. If Hiffs wanted ideas from him, he would suggest making that radio commercial that was bound to be heard in all the apartments in the country within a year's time. And when that project was launched, then on to television. Full of close-ups of girls from early morning on.

He could also handle the more tasteful stuff. After all, the upper middle class was not unfamiliar to him: beauty treatments, new lines of opera glasses, lectures on the fifth and sixth dimensions where promiscuity was a fact of life. Okay, fine! Tom luxuriated in these feeble samples from his storehouse of ideas.

Now that idiot was putting on the brakes again. His gut felt like fresh dough that was rising rapidly. And then they were off again with a vengeance. The guy had no idea how to use the clutch or the brake. The fact that the heat had gradually turned more oppressive didn't make things any better. He simply had to have some fresh air if he wanted to make it. He rolled down his window a crack and felt the humid air blowing down over his face. It felt so good that he pushed himself up in his seat, put his nose all the way over to the opening, and inhaled deeply.

The bus continued in second gear through the tall housing projects outside the city proper. The sidewalks were full of people rushing here and there. On every corner policemen were pressing the buttons that controlled the traffic lights. He ought to make a comment in his novel, when he got that far, about these well-padded policemen who thought they owned the world; these boorish chameleons who befriended the humble and mistreated the indiscreet. Tom began to cough when he saw three policemen on horseback coming up alongside the bus while it was stopped at an intersection. He feared he wouldn't get through town because of the ever suspicious police. Somehow he always managed to look guilty when they were around. They made him stumble over his words so that he couldn't answer properly, and he had to suffer one indignity after another as a result.

Not everyone enjoyed the fresh air as much as Tom did. The women in front of him kept turning around to see where the draft was coming from, and when everyone had noticed, a gray-haired, bespectacled lady said on everyone's behalf, 'There's a draft.'

The driver looked into his mirror from every angle and finally found Tom with his nose up near the opening, inhaling air.

13

'You down there, would you shut the window? The passengers are complaining about the draft,' the driver said.

Tom was far away.

The driver raised his voice a little.

'Would you close that window immediately, please.'

The women began looking back over their shoulders, and the little children started crawling up on the seats and looking down at Tom, who missed the driver's second request. The driver's face had now turned beet-red. The women talked and whispered to one another, and the children asked in loud voices what was wrong with the man who was sticking his nose out the window.

The driver slowed down, pulled over to the curb, and brought the bus to a halt. Then he got up and edged his way down the middle aisle toward Tom, who was terror-stricken when he saw the angry man.

'Would you get off the bus immediately, please,' the driver said.

'But what did I do?' Tom asked cautiously.

'I want you off this minute,' the driver said.

Tom got up and walked down the middle aisle followed closely by the driver. When he reached the door, Tom said, 'What did I do?'

The driver gave him a push. 'Okay, out you go. We don't allow bums here.'

Tom got out and stood on the sidewalk till the bus had disappeared in the traffic.

That bastard was obviously out to show off and take revenge, he thought. Tom quickly started walking toward town, speeding up whenever he passed a policeman. But the third time things went wrong. He accidentally crossed the street at a red light and was called back by the policeman and reprimanded; then he stood there while the light changed to green, yellow, and red without being able to decide whether or not to cross. Finally the policeman came over and said, 'The light's green now. It's okay to cross.'

'Oh, yes,' Tom said and hurried across with the other pedestrians.

He thought about his novel. When he had earned enough money from Hiffs, he would have peace to write a novel. It wouldn't be terribly long, but it would be concentrated, throbbing with insight and prophecy. He would say things, all right, things that would stir up humanity and make the egotists tremble with fear once they realized how they had wasted their lives. It would be the true portrait of an egotist's soul. Pure, unadulterated exposure.

The last one he had written seven years ago had not turned out right. He had felt weaker and weaker, and yet he couldn't stop writing it. It was, to say the least, a mishmash of sentimental slop, but, all the same, he had needed the money since he had borrowed almost as much as he had received for the book, so he had to finish it.

Tom crossed a square where three or four cripples were sitting on folding chairs with their hats on their laps, while a blind man stood near a pissoir singing hymns. He wondered why they all gathered at the same place. Was it just sociability, or were they trying to create a more formidable effect?

'Hey, buddy, got any change?' a man without arms whispered confidentially to Tom as he passed by.

Tom looked down. The man's face was smooth and well-fed, and his smile and his glance shone with malicious glee.

'Hope you get to be a millionaire,' Tom yelled back.

'Thanks,' the man said with a grin.

In the inner city Tom began walking more slowly. He drifted from one second-hand bookstore to the next, pulling books out of their boxes and off the shelves at random, leafing through some of them or just looking to see who had owned the books before, if a signature could be found. Tom was familiar with thousands of books and authors through this sidewalk browsing, which offered him a sentence here, a word there, or just the hint of a mood from the title or the pictures.

It was now past eleven. The newspaper vendors were coming through the streets with the noon papers. Tom bought one and continued his walk through the inner city, reading eagerly. He would stand at crosswalks for several minutes, caught up in his reading until he was awakened whenever someone bumped into him or whenever he felt the scrutinizing glance of women dressed in Persian lamb. Tom recognized a certain intensity in the glance of these women, which hit him hard. It was contempt, rays of contempt.

The noon papers were Tom's favorite reading, although he detested them for being the most revolting things in creation. They wallowed and luxuriated in lechery, sentimentality, scandal, self-righteousness, brutality, banality, whatever, but they did an excellent job, these clever journalists. They knew what people wanted, and they had no qualms about giving it to them. They were impertinent, smutty, blasphemous, but that was, after all, to be preferred to the hypocritical niceties that found their reading public in reactionary circles.

As he passed the cathedral, he was in the process of cramming the paper into one of his coat pockets, but when he didn't succeed immediately, he threw the paper into the gutter. Just at that moment he discovered a picture on the back page that he had not noticed before. He stood there for a long time, guessing his way through the text, which related the story of an eight-year-old Bolivian girl who had just given birth to a child that was reported doing fine. The father was eleven years old. The girl had a touching, imbecile expression on her face and, according to the text, didn't understand what had happened to her. Tom shook his head and kicked the newspaper so that it unfolded and scattered all over the street.

Actually, it was a long time since he had seen Hiffs. Five years or more. He had been together with a journalist who knew Hiffs better, so Tom had held back and only joined in the conversation when a question was directed at him. Because this had probably been the closest he had ever gotten to Hiffs, it was actually hard to understand why Hiffs had called him, unless he had learned a lot about him from someone who knew him well.

But that was neither here nor there. The main thing was that Hiffs felt like seeing him now. Tom was not really surprised. Sooner or later someone like Hiffs would have to realize that he could be useful.

One thought after another crossed Tom's mind, but none remained very long. His consciousness turned in nervous spasms or lost its ability to receive impressions so suddenly that what he had begun to take in died halfway through. His eyes saw, and his ears heard, but the nerve fibers leading inward were blocked by an overwhelming fatigue. The city suddenly didn't exist, nor did he himself. A body without a consciousness was being more or less expertly guided by trained reflexes across squares, through passageways, past monuments.

When Tom awoke from this somnambulant state, his feet had begun to get cold. The dampness from the sidewalk crept up through his soles. He stopped and examined them and, sure enough, found a hole the size of a large coin on the bottom of each shoe. He had felt those holes coming for a long time, but the shoemaker had told him that his shoes were worn out and that they would not support new soles. Now the holes would get larger and larger. There was nothing that could be done about it. He arched his feet, trying to avoid the wet places.

Freezing and shivering in his coat, he wandered across the fish market where the inmates from the mental hospital were sweeping entrails and heads into heaps that were being piled onto small carts pulled up around the square with shaggy, steaming ponies standing in front of them. An inspector wearing a cap, cape, and boots ambled back and forth on the square and kept a hawk's eye on the poor devils to make sure they were doing their job. Tom snorted as he passed him.

Large refrigerated vans were still parked in the streets leading from the square. They were being loaded and unloaded by workers in Icelandic sweaters and bloodstained burlap aprons and with fur-lined caps on their heads. They shouted and snarled at each other or, carrying on conversations, drifted down into murky cellars where there were canteens, blue with tobacco smoke.

Tom suddenly felt like getting warm and slipped down into a coffee bar that smelled of fish and fish oil and sweat and tobacco. It was tightly packed with ruddy-faced men who were talking slowly and looking around as if they trusted no one, while blonde, bosomy, broad-bottomed waitresses in carpet slippers rushed around with fresh provisions.

Tom found himself a place in a corner full of outdoor jackets and hats. The men at the table sent him brief, penetrating glances and continued talking about fish, prices, wind, and weather, as if he didn't exist. When he had been sitting there for twenty minutes without being noticed by any of the waitresses, he came out of his hiding place. He grabbed one of them by the sleeve as she tore by, and she nodded and yelled angrily that she was busy and that surely he could see that and eventually it would be his turn, too.

But it never was his turn. Tom sat for twenty minutes with a cold cigarette in his mouth, intending to save it till his coffee came, but he was ignored. Well, what did he care? He had gotten warm without being dishonest about it, and the coffee didn't really matter since it would probably be awful anyway, judging by the aroma. Three quarters ersatz to one quarter of real coffee. He would have none of it, and he quickly hurried upstairs before one of the buxom girls could catch sight of him.

He came out on one of the major avenues leading down to the large suspension bridge over the river and across it to the affluent quarters in the south end of town. The fog had almost lifted. A thin layer of clouds hanging over the skyscrapers was already giving way to a pervasive lightness that promised blue skies and sunshine, at least for a couple of hours around noon. Toward evening the fog would rise again from the river or come in from the sea.

When he had almost reached the river, he turned into a side street and then immediately to the right. He came out onto a wharfside street whose long expanse was characterized by the motionless avenue of leafless plane trees and countless strolling figures, each with a different tempo.

The street was closed to motor vehicles, and Tom sauntered down the middle of the old-fashioned, uneven pavement where a few leaves that had escaped the street-sweepers' brooms still lay rotting, brown and black, or like fine skeletons stripped of their green flesh. He remembered the years he had lived alone in the city, going about his work as a proofreader or as a substitute at the telegraph office. He especially remembered the summer evenings with their soft light from the north and all the voices under the trees and from the open windows of the houses, where a trumpet now and then would raise its plaintive cry that harmonized so well with what he thought or felt. There had also been a party in one of the studio apartments on the top floor. Hiffs had been there, but he had been in too good a mood to get close to, whereas Tom himself had sat in a corner sipping his drink and laughing whenever the laughter got especially loud. That was probably about ten years ago. Tom began keeping an eye out for Hiffs when he got close to the old pedestrian bridge, whose iron structure now lay ahead of him. It dated from the 1860s and was the first iron bridge built across the river. Farther west, the railroad bridge had then been added, a monster of heavy pylons, most of which surely were not needed.

Tom walked up the stone steps to the bridge and out onto the narrow wooden walkway where only two persons could pass. Out in the middle of it there was a small balcony with a couple of benches with a view to one side. Here he stationed himself, looking down at the river where heavy-laden lighters struggled up against the current on their way inland, where rowboats skimmed across and isolated barges floated rapidly down the grayish-yellow stream.

The vast expanse of huge warehouses and factory buildings rose from the mist far out by the harbor as rays of sunlight broke through here and there, forming glistening patterns on the water or highlighting the coal cranes that moved back and forth, up and down, high above the horizon. Orange peelings glistened as they sluggishly drifted out from under the bridge

19

together with partly rotted cardboard boxes and shards of cinders, and at the edge of the river one of the anglers suddenly lifted his spoon-bait, sending a flash across the river.

Tom stood leaning over the iron railing, which was rough from rust. What he saw was beautiful and unique, but it didn't hold his attention. He slipped into a state of minimal consciousness where the world stared in vain at his inwardness. He stood like that for a long time. His blood ran through him, his muscle fibers quivered, and his nerves made his hands twitch while his feet took turns displaying to the passersby the ragged holes in the soles of his shoes.

A long, narrow, black-tarred boat, a rare type coming from the upper regions of the river, the mountainous regions to the west, emerged from under the bridge. In the center sat a woman completely covered in black with woolen shawls wrapped around her head and shoulders and a bundle in colored cloth on her lap. In the rear of the boat a man was at the helm, a big fellow with a black beard and a white fur cap. Smiling at the man, the woman turned around and said something to him that brought him out of his dream world, and a smile spread from his mouth to his entire face, which had had a touch of gruffness to it.

Just then Tom woke up as he felt someone standing next to him.

He glanced to the side and met a pair of friendly, laughing eyes that rested on him with an expression of quiet inquiry. It was Hiffs.

'Did you see that boat?' Hiffs said. 'It's a rare sight these days. When I was a kid, they used to come all the time. Remember how they came drifting in large flotillas heading for the fall fair, full of cheeses and hams and eggs and live poultry? But maybe you weren't raised here?'

'No,' Tom said. 'I wasn't. I moved here just fifteen years ago.'

They watched the boat as it disappeared under the railroad bridge, and Hiffs began talking about what a fine day it was turning out to be and how he thought they would have some good, warm days now before winter was here for real. Tom listened meekly to his words, which in their banality were charged with a mysterious energy that made the simplest utterance meaningful.

'So,' Tom said, aware that he was being observed. But he could not avoid that forced reticence which always came over him whenever others spoke openly and freely.

'Tom,' Hiffs said, 'how nice that I got hold of you. How are you doing? What are you up to these days? Are you married, divorced, or are you still a bachelor?'

'Well,' Tom said, 'what am I? I guess I'm married.'

'Hm. Doesn't sound to me like you're taking it too seriously,' Hiffs said, laughing. 'Why's that, Tom?'

'Well, I guess you don't really have any idea what you're getting into when you get married,' Tom said. 'Things look altogether different once you have taken the vow.'

'Is that right?' Hiffs said. 'I wouldn't know. Others have said the same thing, but don't you think it's because you chose to ignore a certain part of it before you entered into it? You aren't thinking of getting a divorce, are you?'

'Well . . .' Tom wavered between saying that actually he was, if only he could afford it, or that he would never dream of it because there was no real rift between him and his wife. But that wasn't really it. It was just life in general that wasn't so interesting.

'You don't quite know,' Hiffs said.

'Oh, I don't give a whole lot of thought to it. In the final analysis, it doesn't make any difference. Really, I don't think much about it.'

'It wouldn't be because you don't dare think about it, would it? You seemed to me to be the sort of guy that had dreams of happiness. I mean, don't we all?'

Tom looked at Hiffs, surprised.

'Sure, of course, but honestly, I don't give happiness a thought.'

'But you aren't indifferent either,' Hiffs said.

'No, only kind of.'

'And you seem surprised at the question.'

Hiffs took a pack of cigarettes out of his pocket.

'Thanks,' Tom said, relieved that he could relax a little. There were tensions in his mind over these direct questions, which he wasn't used to and which he wanted to avoid. He didn't like being interrogated, and yet it wasn't really an interrogation. There was nothing humiliating in Hiffs' voice. They just didn't feel the same way about things.

A large blue patch had formed to the south. The mass of light grew noticeably as the sun moved closer, and suddenly the light broke through, strong and hot, and Tom noticed Hiffs standing there squinting, his face to the sun.

A vague nervousness crept into Tom's mind and body. He walked back and forth on the bridge while Hiffs stood there and enjoyed the sun, and it occurred to him that maybe Hiffs had called him just for the fun of it, to kill time or to analyze him. Not that it mattered, but what if he didn't get any money, and what if there wasn't anything at all for him to do? Well, maybe when all was said and done, that didn't make any difference either, but it depressed him nevertheless.

Hiffs turned toward him.

'Aren't you enjoying it?' he said.

'Well, frankly, I'm kind of cold,' Tom said.

'And here I was thinking we could rent a rowboat and take a little trip down the river,' Hiffs said. 'I really felt like it when I saw that boat.'

'I've got a touch of bronchitis, you know,' Tom said. 'I'm almost over it. I don't think sailing would be the best thing for me today. It would have been nice. But you go ahead and go. I'll walk around and wait for you, or I could go in somewhere and wait, or go home.'

'Boy, you really do know how to lie,' Hiffs said cordially. 'But actually, I couldn't care less about that rowboat.'

'Frankly, I don't get any thrill out of rowing on this river,' Tom said. 'There's really nothing to see. Out by the ocean it's something else.'

22

'We could go out there, then,' Hiffs said.

'No, I really can't,' Tom said. 'I've got to be home tonight. I promised. Not too late. And as far as I know, there aren't any trains after nine. But it would have been fun.'

Hiffs stared in amazement at Tom.

'Shall we go back?' he said calmly, but Tom noticed there was something new in his voice, not just composure, but a certain chill. It had come abruptly, and it was impossible for Tom to figure out why, but in any case, he would have to butter Hiffs up so that he would be his friendly old self again.

'This is really a very charming place,' Tom said. 'I used to stand here a lot when I was younger.'

'I saw you here once,' Hiffs said. 'That was before I met you, but you made an impression on me.'

'Really,' Tom said.

'Yes, really,' Hiffs said nodding. 'You're the only person I remember here from the bridge, although I've walked across it many times. I met quite a few girls here. There was almost no way you could get past each other. You'd go first to one side and then to the other, and the other person would do the exact same thing. It always seemed pretty clear to me they simply didn't want to get past, and I always ended up inviting them out somewhere. But with you it was different. I was walking along very slowly one evening, and suddenly someone runs right into me. He just barely turns around and says "Oh" before he is past me. It was you!'

'That's very likely,' Tom said. 'Only I don't remember. As a matter of fact, I've got a pretty bad memory, strange as it may seem. Of course, there are certain things I do remember.'

The police were coming up the river in their patrol boat, its bow dividing the water and creating high crests that eddied into yellow whirlpools in the boat's wake. The officers' caps with their protective covers glistened brightly in the sunshine as the boat swept in under the bridge.

'They're probably going on a picnic in this lovely weather,' Hiffs laughed. 'Did you notice the basket in the middle? I wouldn't want to be in their way when they come back tonight.'

Tom took a couple of turns on the balcony. It all looked hopeless. Hiffs didn't want anything from him after all. All he wanted was to talk and reminisce about the old days; but then, what difference did that make?

'What time has it gotten to be?' Tom said.

'I think it's about twelve-thirty,' Hiffs said. 'You weren't doing anything else, were you, because then I won't keep you. We can always get together some other time.'

'Oh, no,' Tom said. 'This is fine. Of course, I ought to finish that novel of mine so that we can make a little money, but actually I'm not having a whole lot of luck these days. You know how it is, you've always got to warm up one way or the other.'

'Just how far have you gotten?' Hiffs asked.

'Well, I'm about at the halfway mark, about a hundred pages or so.'

'You published a book some years ago, didn't you? Somebody mentioned it. I think I heard it was pretty good.'

'Actually, it was rather unsuccessful,' Tom laughed curtly. 'But I guess you can't sit around forever and pore over the same old story. Sooner or later you have to call it quits and then hope it's accepted. It really doesn't make any difference one way or the other whether it's good or bad, as long as it gets into print. That is, as long as you don't have any ambitions in the way of immortality.'

'And you don't?'

'Are you kidding? I've never been able to afford that kind of thing.'

'Hm.'

'Well, you know, I mean, we're only mortals.'

'Oh.'

'Yeah, you know, those who write for eternity always have an exaggerated opinion of their own importance, don't you think?'

'I guess.'

'I mean, it really bugs me that they're so afraid of lowering themselves.'

'I see what you mean, Tom. You're a realist.'

'Precisely,' Tom said. 'I know what people are like.'

'You know what people are like?' Hiffs said.

'Yeah, kind of,' Tom said. 'All that glitters isn't necessarily gold.'

'No,' Hiffs said and burst out laughing. 'Oh, Tom, the way you talk! How about going back? You're freezing, I can see.'

'I've been sitting inside working for days,' Tom said. 'You get so overly sensitive to cold.'

They strolled toward the south quay with its massive facade of public buildings.

3.

Every so often, gentlemen dressed in black, with bowlers and pointed-toed patent leather shoes, would emerge from the heavy mahogany gates. With measured gait and impeccable posture, they streamed toward the center of town.

Hiffs didn't seem to notice them, but Tom took out his irritation on them by letting out little snorts while secretly hating Hiffs for his total indifference. With righteous indignation he cursed Hiffs for having lured him into town under false pretenses, which was really preposterous when you took into account how busy he was and how necessary it was for him to earn a living. He feared this trip to town would mean something entirely different from what he had hoped for.

To be sure, Hiffs was eccentric, but there was a purpose in what he did. Tom was certain of it. If he didn't really want to use him for something but simply wanted to walk around and yak and question him about this, that, and the other for an entire cold fall day in town, what did he have in mind? Hiffs made use of his days; for that reason he was also making use of this particular day, and Tom was frightened at the thought that no matter how he acted, no matter what he said or didn't say, he was being used, maybe used for something he couldn't grasp, but for something that was in Hiffs' best interest.

What if he were to leave right now? Then that too would be sufficient for Hiffs. Tom didn't doubt it for a moment. He would already have been seen through, weighed, measured, placed, and used for something. This feeling wouldn't let him rest. He rebelled against it, and he silently protested against Hiffs and all his power without being able to utter a word.

'You don't seem to be having a good time,' Hiffs said.

'Oh, I don't know,' Tom said. 'I've gotten kind of spoiled out there in the country. Tramping around town doesn't really do a whole lot for me.'

'If you want to go home, Tom, by all means say so,' Hiffs said.

'Just forget it. Don't give it another thought. Don't you believe for a moment that I'm thinking about it. I just got lost in my own thoughts.'

'So what are you thinking about anyway, Tom?' Hiffs said.

'Oh, I was just thinking how ridiculous it is that a fat cat like the guy we just saw heading for the Chateau Hotel can live high on the hog without doing anything other than tying his shoelaces. I'm telling you, it really bugs me. The guy is stupid. It was obvious. And degenerate, too. Did you get a look at his nose? And they don't even have enough imagination to know how to use their money.'

'Does that really bother you, Tom?'

'Oh, it gets to me once in a while, and then I get furious. Well, not too much, of course. After all, it isn't worth it. I mean, there's no point in wasting your efforts on that sort of thing.'

Hiffs cleared his throat.

Tom felt he had said something stupid, but it made him uncomfortable to be questioned again and again.

'The political aspects of it don't interest me at all,' he said.

'Why not?' Hiffs said.

'They just don't,' Tom said.

'Do you have anything specific against it? Have you looked into what it's all about?'

'It's obviously all money and power,' Tom said.

'And you don't want to have anything to do with that?' Hiffs said.

'No,' Tom said. 'Actually, I don't give it a whole lot of thought. When you have your own business to attend to, then you really don't have the energy to think about politics. It doesn't interest me in the least.'

27

Tom gave Hiffs a quick glance and noticed that he was observing him with a kind of smiling curiosity that might mask something more ominous.

They walked for a while without saying anything and reached the railroad bridge, which continued as a viaduct and railroad embankment between the houses. Just now a diesel switching locomotive, narrow as a radiator, was slowly making its way across it, while the conductor leaned out over the half door.

'Tom, how about getting something to eat?' Hiffs said.

'Sure,' Tom said. 'Fine with me.'

'I know a place that's not too far,' Hiffs said.

Immediately after the viaduct, they turned right, into a wide but short street, which ended in a high, yellow-plastered wall, behind which tall, naked poplars and cypresses could be seen.

'That's the Jewish cemetery,' Hiffs said, and Tom heard him talking about the Jews, their sense of reality, which extended to their faith, their apparent coldness, their passion, their hair color, their big noses, and their delicate hands. Tom could tell that these were personal impressions, observed and contemplated, not mere casual thoughts.

'Sure,' Tom said.

They turned left and wandered into an almost empty street with heavy, damp shadows cast by the five-story, gray cement buildings with their black-glazed mansard roofs. A single van parked outside a cellar was unloading; some children holding hands were standing by a door; a mailman got off his bike, disappeared into a building, returned, got back on his bike, and went on to the next building. The silhouette of a policeman, silent as a statue, could be seen way down the street. It was like walking into death, it seemed to Tom.

'Want to make some money?' Hiffs said.

'Sure,' Tom said, suddenly coming to.

They turned right. An oblique, palpable light shone on the new street, where clusters of women in housedresses stood chatting outside small shops.

28

'Look,' Hiffs said, pointing upward.

'Yeah,' Tom said.

All the windows in the street were open, and in every one of them a woman leaned out, blinking at the sun or calling to children who were playing around in the gutter or rumbling by on roller skates. On one windowsill a black cat was sunning itself among green plants.

'Friendly scene, huh?' Hiffs said.

'Yeah.' Tom couldn't get anything else out. Something went through him in blurry waves. He felt full of energy now that it turned out that he was needed and that he didn't have to concentrate on his own agenda for a while. He was dying to know what Hiffs had in mind, but he couldn't bring himself to ask.

'You almost get the urge to go up and see one of those women, don't you think?' Hiffs said.

'Yeah,' Tom said, paralyzed, but underneath the paralysis something raged in him. He felt that he himself ought to be making a suggestion, and maybe especially now while Hiffs was in a good mood and might dream up any old thing. Tom, too, wanted to say something about the street and the life in it.

'You know, this is really fun,' he ventured self-consciously.

He felt Hiffs' searching glance and endured it. After all, he had to, but he didn't like it. Everyone ought to mind his own business and be able to control his eyes, he thought.

'You know, I've got a lot of great ideas,' he blurted out nervously.

'That right?' Hiffs said, and Tom could hear the amazement in his voice.

'Yeah, you know, it's funny, but I've been thinking for quite some time that I wanted to get hold of you, because I think I've got something that would be right up your alley.'

'Let's talk about it when we get to the restaurant,' Hiffs said.

Tom straightened up in his coat, took in the street scene, and said enthusiastically, 'Hey, this is really a fun street. It's got a real folksy atmosphere about it.'

Hiffs smiled.

The street ended at a round square with four enormous walnut trees surrounded by an iron fence and a few benches. Four double lamps with white globes stood between the trees. The pigeons were hopping about picking grain, which was tossed to them by old, stooped women or by little children in baby buggies, while surly young girls with caps on their heads sat on the benches, rocking the carriages to and fro.

Hiffs stopped and looked at the square while Tom danced around him like a nervous dog. He ran into the fire hydrant, he flicked his hand against the young elm trees that bordered the sidewalk, he cast a quick glance into the little coffee shop, which loomed darkly behind yellow, crocheted lace curtains and square cardboard signs with blue writing on them. It was impossible for him to keep still, though he kept telling himself that he had to, ought to, really must, so as not to irritate Hiffs or in any way make a bad impression. But the moment he thought he was standing absolutely still, he discovered that he was in full motion.

He followed Hiffs as the latter moved on. He would have liked to say something nice about the square, but the imminent discussion made him utterly silent.

'How about sitting down on one of those benches over there?' Hiffs said.

'Sure, fine,' Tom said quickly.

They squeezed in between a couple of young girls rocking baby carriages, and Tom noticed how their glances worked over Hiffs and himself, but not in the same way: hunger and scorn. That part didn't bother him, but it was awful to be sitting down without doing anything. His muscles stiffened, an empty despair came over him, and finally he jumped to his feet.

'Think I'll give my wife a call,' Tom said.

'Fine,' Hiffs said. 'Go ahead. Give her my regards.'

Tom looked for a phone booth and hurried over to the newsstand. He stopped outside and looked at the display of the weeklies with their sickly colors. He lit one of the bent cigarettes he carried in his coat pocket and checked to see if Hiffs had gotten up, but he was still sitting in the same place looking around. Tom walked back and forth, sucking on his cigarette. He had to make a little more time pass.

Finally he marched over to Hiffs and said, 'So, you're still sitting there. I was almost afraid you'd left.'

'Did you get hold of your wife?' Hiffs said, getting up.

'Yeah, you know, I just wanted to let her know I wasn't coming home right away. It's kind of isolated where we live, and she gets a bit anxious. I told her to go ahead and visit her sister.'

'You don't have any children?'

'No, no.'

They cut across to 'The Bagpipe,' a little café with shutters and leaded panes. The smell of oil and a certain stuffy, not unpleasant warmth met them in the small foyer, where they left their coats with an older lady, who spoke with an accent that probably came from the eastern part of central Europe. She was tall and buxom, had black hair and brown, proudly sensual eyes. Her nose was noble and her mouth carefully painted, slightly wide and voluptuous. Hiffs exchanged a few words with her that made her forget her reserve and throw a few cynically provocative remarks in his direction, which made him laugh heartily.

The restaurant was divided into small wooden booths painted brown. Under the low, blue-painted ceiling, there were light fixtures fashioned from wheelbarrow wheels with yellow parchment bracket lamps. The walls were decorated with pictures of Scotsmen and autumn foliage. The floor was covered with red jute runners.

They sat down at a table by the window, and the menu was immediately handed to them by a flatfooted waiter who withdrew a few paces while awaiting his guests' decision.

The restaurant was almost empty: a young couple, an older, white-haired lady with mesh gloves and a pair of glasses dangling on her chest, a couple of well-dressed gentlemen were eating farther inside the restaurant where the overhead light shone white, creating its own separate room.

31

'We'll have a hot meal, what do you say?' Hiffs said.

Tom quickly agreed and heard Hiffs ordering turtle soup and stuffed grape leaves and a bottle of red wine.

'You like that sort of thing?' Hiffs said.

'Yeah, that's fine,' Tom said quickly, waiting for Hiffs to begin their important conversation, but he was busily talking about the room, its height, its breadth, its length, its temperature, its smell, and its acoustics, its furniture, and its clientele, all of which made you feel that the place was especially well suited to taking someone into your confidence, to initiating an intimate, possibly amorous relationship, to striking up a friendship with a lonely lady on a certain sound and respectable plane only to continue it elsewhere. The place seemed peaceful; there was something genuine and straightforward about it, but it lacked any real possibilities for vivacity, for that blissful intoxication. In the long run, one would be likely to feel sluggish with stout here, to talk nonsense, to get drowsy. But for a while, the place might lend a certain gravity to socializing.

Tom was about to pull the tablecloth down onto his lap, but jumped up and got it pulled back in place without Hiffs' giving it a second glance. He lit a cigarette and inhaled deeply to soothe his nerves. If only he would be allowed to talk. He felt a cold streak of perspiration trickling down his spine, but he didn't know if he had it in him anymore to come up with any suggestions.

'Hey, Hiffs?' he managed to get out after the next pause.

'Yeah,' Hiffs said. 'What is it you're so anxious to tell me? Make yourself comfortable, Tom. Enjoy yourself, relax. Here comes the red wine.'

Tom leaned back on the couch and watched the waiter place the glasses and pour as if it were a sentence that had been imposed upon him.

'To you,' Hiffs said.

'Cheers,' Tom said, taking a big swallow.

'Now, then. What was it you wanted to tell me?' Hiffs said, looking at him.

'Oh, that can wait until later,' Tom mumbled. 'We're having such a good time right now.'

'Yeah, could be worse,' Hiffs said.

Tom played with his glass and lifted it to see how the red wine would look through the facetting of its foot, but he barely raised it high enough, before the glass returned of its own accord, and he picked up the half cigarette he had placed on the edge of the ashtray and lit it with difficulty. Hiffs was probably taking it all in, he thought.

'I think I've gone bananas,' he said.

Hiffs continued looking at him, and Tom felt that he hadn't said enough and that he could go ahead and say more.

'Frankly, I live a rotten life,' he said. It was clear that Hiffs was listening carefully.

'I'm not making any money at all.'

Hiffs smiled, and Tom noticed that this time it was with scorn.

'Well, maybe it's my own fault.'

Hiffs continued to smile. He looked as if he were thinking: I've heard that one before.

'I guess it doesn't do a whole lot of good to be aware of it,' Tom said, wanting to appeal to Hiffs' sympathy at any cost.

'No,' Hiffs said. Tom was silent because maybe Hiffs wanted to add something.

'You know, I have an idea,' Tom said aggressively. 'I'm sure you can do something with it. How about building an international hotel, a radio transmitter and commercial station, a casino, and a variety theater on a huge liner, which could be moored just outside the three-mile limit? I'll bet you there's money in it. It's a fantastic idea. I know I'm not the only one who has thought of it. After all, there's nothing new under the sun. And I'm only telling you because it's just the kind of thing you could do something with. Nothing to it. A real treat. There's not a company that wouldn't want to advertise. And no censorship. What you couldn't do on a boat like that. In fact, that's actually the question, I mean, if one boat would be enough. Before you know it, you'd have a whole fleet with cruise passengers aboard, ready to try out your swanky facilities. But, of course, I leave it up to you.'

'I'm afraid it won't work,' Hiffs said.

'Well, then,' Tom said, downing some wine, 'in that case there are so many other things. Did it ever occur to you that one could try making a little plastic lunch box with individual compartments that you could put bread, butter, and different kinds of sandwich fixings in? Everything arranged separately. You could make your sandwich with your pocket knife, or with a knife at the office, or with an accompanying neat little plastic knife, and you wouldn't have to eat that nasty, soggy sandwich which half the population brings from home and is forced to swallow every single day. I'm telling you, I often thought about that kind of lunch box when I used to work in the editorial office. Cheaper and better than *smørrebrød* and fresher and better for you. You could hook up with a bakery, a dairy, a butcher, a truck farmer. That way you could get the ingredients cheap. All you'd have to do is get it going; after that, it'll take care of itself. Why should anyone carry a lunch? Don't you think it makes sense? We'll deliver your daily lunch for less than you can make it yourself — and fresher and healthier at that. Don't you think . . . I mean, it sounds downright tempting. Then there would be vitamin charts on the box so that people would know it's good for them. Hell, who cares if it's true or not. Good Lord! And then you'd have to have a low-calorie lunch with a calorie chart. You'd sell millions of them. Let's face it, people want the whole works ready-made in a box these days.'

'Not a bad idea, Tom,' Hiffs said. 'Not a bad idea at all.'

'Like it?' Tom said, running his fingers along the edge of the table. He had to touch something. His exaltation had carried him so far away and so high up. Delighted, he looked at Hiffs, but couldn't figure him out. Would he buy the idea? Was he sitting there trying to figure out what it would cost?

'Personally, that's the only kind of lunch I would have in my house,' Tom assured him.

'Are you serious?' Hiffs said.

Tom nodded.

'Sure. What are you going to do with all those leftovers? Who feels like figuring out how much he needs? I mean, let others do the thinking for you. Then you're free to think about something else.'

Tom laughed, but he knew he was perspiring hard. He was exhausted. Now it was Hiffs' turn.

'Not a bad idea at all,' Hiffs said.

'Listen to me, Hiffs,' Tom said, sitting up on the couch, 'the way things are today, people don't like packing their own lunches, and they can't afford to go out to eat that expensive *smørrebrød*. We'd be helping them out of their dilemma, don't you see? We have simply heard the subconscious voices of the times demanding it, and now we're able to provide it. I know it sounds strange to use those phrases, but I'm telling you, there's a need for it. Damn it, there's a need for it. Pardon me if I say so myself, but I do think it's a great idea, and, sure, people can buy bread, and butter, and cold cuts separately, but the fact that the butter and the bread and the cold cuts are all made for each other, the fact that it's all just the right amount, that's what this generation can't resist. That's obvious. And you could make similar combinations for breakfast and dinner. A housewife wouldn't have to think at all, and she wouldn't have to run around from one store to another.'

Hiffs said, 'Not a bad idea, as I told you, not at all. You don't have any others?'

'This is my best one.'

'I see, but tell me about some of the others, just briefly, if you don't mind.'

'I don't know, I've got so many it's almost impossible to keep them all straight. I can shake them out of my sleeve anytime I want to, I'm telling you. Ideas won't let me rest. I can't go for a walk without three or four of them popping into my head. I should probably have someone write them down for me, that's how fast they come. But just at the moment, I have zeroed in on those two; the others, well, I've got to give a little more thought to them before I'm ready to pass them on.'

Tom took the ashtray and turned it in his hands.

'No, Hiffs, this is the best I've got, but if you want some more, it won't take me long to dream up something really super.'

'Who do you have in mind to sell your idea to, Tom?'

Tom gasped for breath, he was getting dizzy, and he fell back on the couch. He kept hearing Hiffs' voice repeating the same words over and over again.

'Well, frankly, I haven't given that a whole lot of thought,' he stammered.

Hiffs' voice spoke again. 'I see.'

It was disinterested, Tom could tell, a bit callous, judgmental, as it had been that time on the bridge, but then it had soon been all right again.

Tom straightened up and flapped his hands.

'The trouble is, I've lost my connections. As you well know, all the old boys are sitting in their soft desk chairs doing useful stuff. They don't have too high an opinion of me. They're afraid I'm going to show up and ask them to read one of my stories. So I would just as soon not approach them. But there are supposed to be agencies for that sort of thing, so, frankly, I had thought of going to see them one of these days. A naive meat packer is always good for a hundred kroner.'

'And do you know any naive meat packers?' Hiffs said.

'Well, no, but as you and I both know, they're all so dumb you can talk them into anything, and a hundred kroner doesn't mean a thing to them.'

Hiffs looked at Tom.

'Just what is it you're after, Tom?' he said.

'Well, you know, you've got to get some money together; you've got to keep at it, and you can't. It's harder than hell.'

'I can get you a job,' Hiffs said.

'Really?' Tom said, suddenly unable to breathe.

'A friend of mine needs to have a whole bunch of documents copied. You do type?'

36

For a moment the image of the restaurant had been sharp and clearly outlined for Tom in the most minute details. Now it was torn to shreds, and he kept hearing the biting scorn in Hiffs' voice. He felt his life being crushed into nothingness. He desperately searched his soul for a corner where he could hide from this voice that insisted on driving him out, that wanted to set him in motion, that in the final analysis wanted him to live, and he didn't have the strength. Every step would be like walking on razor blades. He groaned inwardly at the thought of some routine slavery that would make an ordinary human being out of him, or a man with one less excuse. The excuses were to be reduced, and finally he was to embark on the positive path. Maybe it was his own wild imagination, but Hiffs' voice was like that. It would always remain decidedly sharp even when he was thinking up some crazy scheme or other. That Tom was sure of.

Slowly he relaxed, and, trying to smile, he said, 'Well, that's a good idea.'

'Yeah, don't you think?' Hiffs said.

'No,' Tom said shaking his head. 'I can't. I've got my novel, you know. There's no way. It can't be done. I know it's a cop-out, but I'm almost forty. I can't change, Hiffs. It was nice of you to think of me, but I really can't commit myself.'

'Whatever you say,' Hiffs said. 'It's not every day a job like that comes along.'

'Don't give it another thought,' Tom said. 'I'll be all right.'

Tom was quite cheerful over the fact that he had gotten out of it.

'You wouldn't happen to have some cigarettes?' Tom said.

Hiffs placed a pack on the table, and Tom tore it open and fished out a cigarette.

'So, how are things with you?' Tom said. 'Any new projects?'

'Projects?' Hiffs said puzzled.

'Well, I take it you're up to something or other, or don't you feel like it anymore?'

Hiffs shook his head.

37

'Oh, so you're simply taking it easy,' Tom said with a little laugh. 'Guess you've raked in enough money to enjoy life. You've been smart, Hiffs, really clever . . .'

'What do you mean?' Hiffs said.

'Well, at least you've gotten something out of it. Everything has come your way, and there you sit, content, independent, and can laugh at it all.'

'I don't think that's the entire story,' Hiffs said. 'But maybe that's how it looks. Tom, you believe in money, don't you? I never did. To me it has never been anything but numbers on paper.'

'Just why did you call me?' Tom said, laughing nervously.

'To talk to you, Tom,' Hiffs said, and Tom heard the voice sounding fatally hard again.

'Sure,' he said. 'You know, I read in the paper about an eight-year-old girl, from Bolivia or Colombia, who had a child with an eleven-year-old boy. They start early down there; they develop early, she didn't know what it was all about. Oh, well, it's probably all lies anyway.'

'It's impossible for you to understand that I want to talk to you,' Hiffs said, moving his chair back as the waiter came and began serving the soup.

Tom thought for a long time, so long that he had begun to forget what it was he was supposed to reply to.

'Yes,' he finally said.

He looked at Hiffs, who burst out laughing heartily.

4.

'How well I know you again, Tom,' Hiffs said. 'I'm sure it must be sheer hell for you to sit still and listen to me. I have a way of shutting you up. That's the way I remember you from the few times we met before. You were sitting in a corner, fearful, almost careworn, and had no choice but to despise it all because you didn't feel you were able to play the game. There was something cold and aloof about you that made you seem unapproachable, but that's what piqued my curiosity. Once in a while I'd see you flare up for a moment, like a caged bird that wants to fly, and I knew you would make some suggestion or other that would sever your chains for good, that would liberate you from those forces within you that weighed upon you like an evil, oppressive rock of fatigue, a despondency, a coma. You never seriously believed it, but I could tell you glimpsed it in dream-like flashes. If you had been serious about it, it probably would have happened, but it was as if you were better suited to this little misfortune which, I guess, has not gotten either smaller or larger since the last time we met. Actually, that's what I wanted to know. That's why I called.'

Tom put down his spoon and sat back on the couch.

'No, no, no,' Hiffs said. 'Go right ahead and eat. After all, it's just the truth I'm telling you. Don't let that distract you. Does it mean anything at all that I'm telling you this?'

Tom smiled wistfully.

'I knew you wanted to talk about the ideas you had, but my God, Tom, lots of people have good ideas. It was naive of you, and still is, to think that yours are so unique. I could have all the ideas I want. And why didn't I pick up on yours? I think I owe you an explanation.

'I wanted to see how you would manage without being given a break, Tom. All the others who were not given a chance with me tried their luck elsewhere. I guess you did, too, but not with the same intensity. There was something so indifferent, so rolled out about you, Tom, that it had to be attempted, it had to be turned into a life story. I see that's what it has become. You're just the way you were then.'

'Yeah, it's been a real mess, all of it,' Tom said shaking his head. 'Guess I haven't exactly turned out right.'

'Only it hasn't had any effect on you,' Hiffs said. 'That's what I wanted to know. There are others, Tom, who when they become aware of their misfortune or their failure, straighten out, change, or jump off a bridge, hang themselves from a tree, take a pill, put their heads in the oven; or they grieve the rest of their lives, live in the blinding spotlight of sorrow, bitterness, or madness; they see themselves forever as incomplete human beings, as stunted individuals, as invalids. But not you! I've got a theory about you.

'You're invulnerable, Tom, because you're proud. There's no point in telling you this, because you always find a new corner to retreat to. Your soul is not a place, a source of strength; yours is the empty conch in which you can hear the roaring of your distant, invincible pride. It's a complex pride, an unusual pride, maybe it's called something else, but I haven't been able to come up with a better word for this extraordinary ability of yours to evade life.

'Others would call this a day of reckoning, but I knew that for you that wouldn't be the case. I know, of course, that it hurts a little; after all, you still have a trace of your parents' bourgeois morality in you, but the person that's truly you, Tom, doesn't really resent what I'm saying.'

'Just what are you getting at?' Tom said. 'Was that really the only reason you called me?'

'Not entirely,' Hiffs said. 'But almost.'

'Then I guess I might as well go home,' Tom said.

'All right, but you aren't going to, are you?' Hiffs said.

'Guess I'm still hoping,' Tom said.

'For what?' Hiffs said. 'I can't use your ideas.'

'Why not? They're just as good as anybody else's.'

'They don't mean anything to you. If they really meant something to you, I would make something out of one of them for you.'

'The thing is, I don't have a dime to my name, Hiffs.'

'You'll think of ways, Tom. You don't have any attachments.'

'But my wife, Hiffs.'

'Just send her off to her sister's. What's your wife to you anyway? She's just a stumbling block that life has placed in your path. Not anything you ever wanted. You could probably stay with her sister, too, for a while, until you talked someone into lending you a hundred kroner.'

'Just why have you been play-acting like this?'

'Play-acting, you say? I wanted to talk to you. I don't think it humiliates you. It's you who have been mistaken, Tom. I have nothing to do with ideas anymore. I've unloaded all my business concerns. I'm not doing anything special.'

'You've turned to psychology instead, then?'

'Call it what you like. Here I am. Here you are. Isn't that enough?'

'How can you be so sure of yourself?'

'Contradict me, Tom. I'd just as soon be proven wrong. Why am I so sure? I'm not sure. I say what comes to mind to give you a chance to contradict me. But you don't contradict me.'

'Frankly, I don't feel like it,' Tom said, smiling as best he could.

'Contradict me, Tom,' Hiffs said. 'It's important to me.'

'Why important to you? I should think you couldn't care less. After all, you're so sure of yourself.'

Hiffs frowned and finished his soup.

'It's cold,' he said, 'but good. Do you like turtle soup?'

41

'Sure,' Tom said. 'Nothing wrong with that.'

Tom fished out a cigarette and lit it. He noticed that his hands were shaking, but otherwise he was all right. After all, what Hiffs had said was old news; he knew it all himself; it stung a little more to have it presented by an outsider, but he had been the first to see his own faults.

A heavy-set gentleman came in through a door in the back of the room, opened up the piano with a bang, sat down, put his head to one side and then back a little, and began playing a sentimental piece that made Hiffs prick up his ears, while Tom felt it was getting easier to talk; sentimentality always loosened your inhibitions.

He began humming a little to himself, but when he saw Hiffs looking at him, he stopped and said with a dry laugh, 'Know what, Hiffs? A guy ought to live like this every day. All we need here is to have the room packed with fat, long-haired women and skinny, short-haired ones, the serious, anemic type, all joined in heart-rending sentimentality.'

'Would you know anything about that?' Hiffs said.

'No, no,' Tom said, 'but I have a feeling that's how it would be. Look at those two young people over there. I mean, really! Well, I guess that's their business.'

'This is the kind of music that's well aware of the effect it has,' Hiffs said. 'It knows the human heart, and it knows what it takes to move you. If you'll notice, it doesn't create fullness in your heart, it doesn't make you wise or decisive; it creates emptiness, longing, immaturity, so that the girls are taken in by the first, velvety-soft glance that comes their way. It erases differences, forms soft, warmish hazes and clouds of people; it is wet, clammy, it shuns the fire. It's music that can seduce a tailor's daughter. By the way, do you know anything about modern music?'

'Don't tell me you've started going to concerts, Hiffs?'

'I haven't done anything else for the last three years.'

'But the audience! How do you stand it?'

'What difference does that make? You're letting the little

things get to you, Tom, because there's nothing you really enjoy. With people like you around, there would be no one to climb Mount Everest for us. There's a natural order to things when you want something.'

'You're really marvelously wise, Hiffs,' Tom said. 'I had no idea that's what you were getting at.'

'You don't believe there are any values, Tom. But there *are* values; we would have chaos in the world if we didn't order it according to the values it holds for us. But I guess you don't concern yourself with that sort of thing. You don't have to worry.'

Hiffs raised his glass in a toast. Tom took a swallow.

'You know, you really are quite conceited, Hiffs,' he said.

Hiffs smiled.

'What fancy phrases you come up with! Sounds expensive!'

'You're right, Tom; that's what's been on my mind lately.'

'All right!'

They touched glasses.

'Frankly, I think you've started taking things much too seriously,' Tom said. 'What's all that claptrap you went on about really supposed to mean? I mean, I already know all that garbage; it's the same old stuff, as you well know. What's the point? You aren't by any chance going through some kind of personal crisis? Because I sure don't see what you want with me today.'

'I wanted to talk to you. I already told you,' Hiffs said.

'Oh, come on,' Tom said. 'You just wanted to see what effect it would have on me, and I guess you got what you wanted. Are you satisfied now? Do you want me to leave, because maybe you have others lined up, waiting to go through the same kind of rigmarole? Just what's your game, Hiffs?'

'I want to give you ten thousand kroner, Tom,' Hiffs said.

Holding on to the edge of the table, Tom stumbled to his feet.

'What did you say?' he said in a hoarse voice.

'I want to give you ten thousand kroner,' Hiffs said.

'Well,' Tom said. He felt relieved yet physically squeezed,

compressed to the point of explosion. He would have to have the money right away if it were to do him any good. He would have to leave, get out of there, take a cab home, give Etna the money, go out for another walk. He couldn't stand waiting, he read it in Hiffs' face, which was intently turned in his direction so as to observe his feelings while at the same time covering up new surprises. He had to sit down whether he liked it or not. He had to have a cigarette.

'I won't give it to you now,' Hiffs said.

'No,' Tom said, throwing the match in the ashtray.

'There are conditions,' Hiffs said.

'I figured that,' Tom said, already beginning to nod off with exhaustion at the very thought of what he might be expected to do and perhaps wouldn't be able to carry out.

'It's easy work,' Hiffs said. 'Or rather, it's no work at all.'

Tom had slumped back on the couch and was staring in the direction of the piano player, who in some absurd way, it seemed to him, was playing soundlessly as if on a silent piano.

'I want you to write something that's real,' Hiffs said.

'What do you mean by that?' Tom said. 'Are you thinking of publishing it?'

'That's not the point,' Hiffs said. 'Did you hear what I said?'

'Sure,' Tom said. 'Something real. Does it have to be long?'

'Long enough,' Hiffs said. 'Neither too long nor too short. The length doesn't matter.'

'Would a couple of hundred lines do?' Tom said.

'Why not?' Hiffs said. 'That's not what matters. The only thing is, it has to be real. Know what I mean? It has to be a real, true experience. It sounds lofty, but I can't demand less. Every word must be true.'

'Who will be the judge?' Tom said.

'I will,' Hiffs said. 'You'll get the money the moment I've read it.'

The waiter was suddenly standing by the table.

'Certainly, go ahead,' Hiffs said. 'We're finished with the soup. And bring us another bottle.'

44

The waiter began clearing the table.

The piano player was in the process of hammering out a dramatic passage. His shoulder blades moved up and down under his black coat in little jerks, which apparently fascinated the old lady immensely. She sat there as if mesmerized by this special accompaniment, while the two businessmen talked louder and louder and kept bursting out in raucous laughter as they put their heads close together and gazed into each other's eyes. The two young people were enjoying themselves. The girl had her head on the man's shoulder, and once in a while he would stroke her wispy hair, or he would smile down at her whenever he could tear himself away from his beer bottle, which he contemplated constantly while caressing it with light strokes.

'Looks like they're having a good time,' Hiffs said to Tom. 'He has no idea what to say to her, but she's enjoying herself anyway. People generally don't need too many words; they let themselves be transported by an instinctive peace of mind radiating from another human being. They rest by each other's side and breathe lightly, as if in a lovely landscape: a tree, a rock, a spring. Words only get in the way when the sense of touch is intact and fully activated. What does it mean to be an intellectual other than to have lost one's capacity to feel, to touch, to have a need for these things? When one can live entirely on an abstract plane where words are no longer sounds, perceptions, but only meanings and finally only signs within a world of symbols in the chess game of abstract thought, then one is an intellectual – and even on that plane one finds courage and cowardice, audacity and caution. I think, Tom, that at one time these abstractions were towers where you could rest and from which you could survey the concrete world; I think they were considered mighty resting places, sometimes fortresses that were impregnable but that could never form the nucleus of human existence. It was only later that we put this remoteness into our very existence, where the sense of touch is so invaluable if we're not to transform most of our lives into meaningless gestures.'

Tom shook his head.

'I don't know about you, Hiffs. I'm about to lose respect for you. If only I could. I think everything you say sounds ridiculous, and yet I don't believe you're just putting on an act. But you come close. I mean, you're full of fancy phrases, pure nonsense. Just what are you getting at?'

'Why are you getting so upset?'

'Oh,' Tom said grimacing, 'it really doesn't upset me. I just don't think you need to go on and on about it. You've got money. You can do whatever you want. Just why are you living in the city anyway?'

'Actually, I'm not. I live in a house on the beach. I came into town to talk with you, and so here I am, talking to you about different thoughts I've had. But is there actually anything else to discuss? I've told you what I wanted to tell you. You've heard it. That's what I had in mind.'

'When do you want the stuff I'm supposed to write?'

'In two days, in three days, preferably within a week. But I'm sure you work fast, so that should be easy. I'll write down my address for you, then you can come on out and drop it off.'

'What are you going to do with it?'

'Look at it.'

'Why?'

'I just want to. But don't ask so many questions, Tom. Now it's your turn to come through. Is this what you expected?'

'Frankly, no,' Tom said. 'And do I get the money right away?'

'Yes,' Hiffs said, 'if what you write is real, then you'll get the money right away.'

'You couldn't let me have an advance?' Tom said.

'No.'

'To tell you the truth, we've got nothing to heat the house with, Hiffs,' Tom said. 'It can't make a whole lot of difference to you. A hundred kroner is enough. Let me have a hundred kroner, Hiffs, for God's sake, you'll have it back if I don't . . .'

'No,' Hiffs said, 'that I can't agree to.'

'Okay,' Tom said. He shook a new cigarette out of the pack

and lit it. He began to cough, continued coughing, had a real coughing fit, which left him with a red face and watery eyes.

'Damn it all,' he said, trying to be more cautious about puffing on his cigarette. He would have to watch that he didn't inhale too deeply.

The waiter placed a new bottle of red wine on the table, and Hiffs immediately filled their glasses.

'Better have something for your throat,' he said.

Tom cleared his throat.

They touched glasses.

'I've seen you drunk only once, Tom,' Hiffs said. 'You were completely out of it. You started attacking a girl who then pushed you away so that you landed in an armchair. There you remained completely stiff until you finally fell to the floor, where you stayed for about an hour. Then you got up and staggered through the apartment, holding on to the walls and the furniture, without saying a word. You just kept walking. Finally you got a ride home with some other people. You probably don't remember.'

'I wonder why I was invited in the first place?' Tom said.

'They thought you had talent; and so it seemed a shame for you always to be by yourself. If you hadn't had any talent, then it wouldn't have mattered so much. It's a strange mentality, but actually that's the way people think. There's nothing harder than to see through a helplessness like yours and not attribute to you a number of other mysterious qualities to try to make up for it. People can be more compassionate than you might think when they want to be; they have faith in the misfits. They always think something is bound to come of them.'

'It wasn't all fun and games for me,' Tom said, 'in case that's what you're thinking.'

'I guess it wasn't much different from anything else in your life. And you know that very well yourself. Was it any better to be alone? I wonder. After all, better to suffer in the company of others as long as there was heat, food, and drink. But you've gotten married in the meantime. I'm surprised, and yet I'm not.

47

I can imagine how it happened, and it's probably no worse for you than not being married. It's all the same. But I guess you admitted that yourself.'

'Why did you give up all your business ventures?' Tom said.

Hiffs thought a little.

'One weekend I went out to my house on the coast. The weather was great. I went sailing, I went swimming. On Monday morning the weather was even better. I stayed on. Tuesday better still. Why not stay? Wednesday it rained. I called my secretary and told her that I was getting out. I stayed where I was, and that's where I've been ever since. It's never taken me long to make up my mind, Tom. I've done what was right in front of my nose. If you do that, everything else takes care of itself. You simply follow everything closely. Asserting your will really doesn't get you too far. A strong will makes even the lighter things heavy, the thinnest things impenetrable. But if you stand back, then things open up by themselves. You don't have to believe. You can be quite confident that nothing is impossible. That's what I've always counted on. It has baffled others who had strong wills but who were stuck in a rut. When you consider problems easily solvable, then they usually are. After all, it's not a matter of kicking your way through the heavy gates of difficulty but of finding the light, unlocked back door where you can simply walk right in. A sense of the undramatic can spare you a lot of grief. There's really nothing we're obliged to do here in life; no one is telling us what to do. So it's probably best to follow those courses of energy that crop up and develop and not attribute too much importance to ourselves. One must simply seize the moment, that's a condition for this kind of existence.

'For the past three years now I've lived slowly, exceedingly slowly and followed my own design insofar as that was possible. I've walked along the coast for days without turning back; I've slept in guard houses or broken into summer houses; I've been out on the ocean in my boat without doing anything at all other than drift with the current until the course was run and I felt like returning to my house again. It has been a time clear as day. I've spent very little time thinking; I've existed among things. There's thought in that, too, but it's a concrete, living thought that keeps unfolding. Music has given me a lot; reality is changed definitively when you're in touch with everything that streams through the ear.

'The other day I happened to think of you, Tom, and since I was in town anyway, I decided to give you a call.

'Hmm, I wonder what's keeping the food?'

'It sounds like you've been happy,' Tom said. 'It's really fantastic, you know, but you've had a real knack for it.'

'Here's the food,' Hiffs said.

The waiter served the dolmas, which lay in a gleaming mound together with rice, fresh tomatoes, and slices of pineapple.

'Like this sort of thing?'

'Sure,' Tom said, watching the waiter's hand as it busily heaped large spoonfuls on his plate. 'Thanks. That's plenty.'

'I take it you don't care that much about food,' Hiffs said.

'No, not really. I don't usually eat that much.'

Hiffs shook his head. 'A wonder you're still alive.'

'Well, I don't know,' Tom said. 'It's not because of anything I did. But I'm not the type to commit suicide. What good would it do? Nothing is that unpleasant. Even suicide is not that unpleasant, but there's something dramatic about it. You'd have to be taking yourself pretty seriously, it seems to me. I'm really not up to it.'

'Who knows if you aren't cheating yourself, Tom,' Hiffs said. 'Maybe some deep-seated morality is preventing you from doing so. Are you fond of your wife?'

'Hm, how can I answer that; after all, you're together day in and day out. It's a real drag. I don't know, maybe I am fond of her. I don't really know. It gets a bit old.'

Hiffs got up and headed for the door at the back of the room.

Tom sat hunched over and stared at the pattern of the chair and table legs. He felt surprisingly good and kept mumbling to himself, we'll soon see to that, we'll soon see to that, while images and bits of images flowed through him with the broad rhythm of a river. Ten thousand kroner was a lot of money, a lot of money, but what would he do with it? He would be forced to complete his house, and once in it he would walk around like his own prisoner, have good manners hammered into him, be forced to work. Maybe a child would even be demanded of him, which it would be impossible for him to produce, and after countless scenes he would be obliged to adopt a kid and now be forced to love two persons, both of whom he couldn't care less about. Two persons; everything indicated that that was even worse than one unless, of course, the two of them got along. Maybe then he would be off the hook. Maybe then he could simply up and leave. And, of course, come back again, because what was the point of leaving? He didn't need the ten thousand, and still he felt that it had its own purpose. He couldn't help going for it. And then the assignment was so easy. Something real! Good Lord! All he had to do was write about a visit to the grocery store and all the spite and sarcasm that went with it. That was reality. That's how human beings behaved. Or the bus driver! That's how human beings behaved. Or the cripples! That's the way they were.

With ten thousand kroner he could pay all the bills, but that wasn't too much fun either. He could blow it, of course; after all, no one would know that he had made that much money. But blow it on what? He could spend ten kroner, but ten thousand, that was a thousand times too much. He could invite people over, but there was no joy in celebrating with people whose appetite for life was much larger than your own. That only made you silent and hollow. Melancholy was more fun. For example, wasn't Etna easier to deal with when she was in tears? Then there was something to say to her. All you had to do was comfort her and pretend you cared. But what to do with her if she were happy? Tom felt he could be thrown completely off balance just by seeing someone else happy.

Hiffs returned.

'We'll have to dig in; otherwise the food will get cold.'

They ate in silence. The piano player had started playing a lively Viennese waltz. Now and then he would smile at the old lady who furtively kept an eye now on the piano player, now on a young couple. The two parties might even be in league, since every time the piano player began a new piece, he seemed to strike the very mood that tended to increase the couple's state of infatuation, while the sensitive, somewhat heavy-set piano player for his part was tempted to heighten their passion even further.

The waiter was stationed by the column in the middle of the room. He was watching the two businessmen, who had become secretive now and alternately spoke in hushed and loud voices while stirring their coffee again and again to dissolve the imaginary sugar.

Tom lit a cigarette.

'Aren't you going to have any more?' Hiffs said.

Tom shook his head.

'Me neither,' Hiffs said. He looked in the direction of the waiter.

'May I have the check, please,' he said in a loud voice.

The waiter was at their table in no time. He bowed politely.

'I was going to give you my address, Tom,' Hiffs said, getting out a pen and a note pad.

'Yeah, thanks,' Tom said.

Hiffs paid the waiter, wrote his address on a slip of paper, and handed it to Tom.

'Ready to leave?' he said to Tom. 'You probably have a lot to do. I imagine you have to get home and get to work.'

Tom edged out of the couch. Hiffs suddenly seemed reserved.

The cloakroom lady smiled from afar as they emerged from the dining room. She chattered away, but Hiffs answered in monosyllables and got his coat so fast that he was already waiting outside the door by the time Tom had gotten his.

'I'm going that way,' he said, pointing to the right. 'You're

51

probably going left to get home quickly. It was nice talking to you, Tom. I hope you'll be in touch before long. You can ask for directions at the station.'

'Couldn't you just let me have enough for the fare?' Tom said. 'To tell you the truth, I can't really afford it.'

'Here's thirty kroner, Tom.' Hiffs yanked a few bills out of his coat pocket. 'Bye now, and take care. I'll be waiting to hear from you.'

He nodded and started walking.

Tom rolled up the bills and put them in the inside pocket of his overcoat. At least he had gotten a little something out of it.

He took the direct route down to the river.

5.

Tom stopped in the middle of the large suspension bridge and lit a cigarette. He happened to have put Hiffs' cigarettes in his own pocket, but Hiffs wouldn't think ill of him for that. After all, he didn't smoke.

The traffic streamed by in a tight, slow caravan that was being squeezed out of the center of town. The pedestrians on the sidewalks had their coats open, and the young women had thrown theirs over their shoulders and were walking with half-closed eyes, enjoying what might be the last sunshine of the fall.

Tom walked back and forth for a while along the marble balustrade and looked down toward the pedestrian bridge whose balconies were crowded with people adjusting their binoculars or holding up their children so that they could watch the life on the river. All this was real, all right, Tom said to himself. All he needed to do was to record his impressions accurately, then he would have solved the problem. Or he could write about the buses, the trucks, and the irate sports cars that roared impatiently in the traffic snarls. It was just a matter of calling things by their right names, then he would be ten thousand kroner richer. And yet, it was as if he couldn't sanction this decision, the idea that he was standing in the middle of reality. It was a general supposition, he knew, that what could be located physically was real, but he felt that all those things people were spending endless energy on maintaining, regulating, and controlling could vanish from his consciousness and pale before his eyes until they no longer existed. He could stare at a car, but just as it was sitting there – dark, palpable, and like something that tormented his consciousness – it would start to crumble, but the stream of his consciousness kept moving, relieved and unreal.

These young women, whose sweaters and blouses were so low-cut that you began to glow in the splendor and warmth of their skin when you passed them, and who then disappeared with their supple backs, their pale perfumed necks under long hair or voluptuous knots, with their elegantly swaying hips, which made the room sway, feminine around them, with their nimble legs and feet, which stepped so confidently, gracefully, dazzlingly on the ground – did they exist for any other reason than for that tepid, brief infatuation that circulated through the branches of your nervous system only to leave it exhausted and spent? At what point did the road lead to the reality of all this that called itself reality, but that was just matter fading into grayness and languor the moment the senses lost their immediate contact?

Tom followed the avenue, and at first he distinctly noticed these steep surfaces that meant buildings, these interruptions that meant cross streets, squares, these buzzing obstacles that meant people; all this unreality he was conscious of in a manner of speaking, but gradually this alternate state of his deteriorated, and he walked again like a being that didn't exist but merely moved like a shadow across undetermined distances.

In this condition, he reached the bus station just as his bus was pulling away from the platform. He tried waving to the driver, who shook his head unsympathetically. He loitered on the platforms, whose wire baskets were full of paper and orange and banana peels, their benches with postered backs, and their scales, which hefty women stepped up on whenever they thought no one was watching. The buildings rose thirteen stories high above the square, which was cold and gloomy even on a day like this.

Tom went into the cafeteria with its stale air and its many faces, which suddenly looked up at him from their stoneware cups, its long stainless-steel counter, where a pale, hollow-eyed fellow was squeezing the handle of the espresso machine, turning around automatically when Tom opened his mouth to order coffee; with its shelves of greenish, yellowish, and reddish soda pop in nubbly bottles, its battalions of Coca-Cola, its juke box shimmering with plexiglass and smoldering perversely with neon, while its thirty-six records rested like a stack of dishes after a bash.

Tom gulped down his coffee while casting a sidelong glance at a couple of fellows who were sitting at a table rolling dice out of a leather cup. They didn't talk, didn't call out the numbers, but simply pushed the cup across the table after shaking it three times. They were men in their thirties with a kind of shabbily well-dressed look about them: striped ties with a spot here and there, plaid suits that looked as if they had been bought at a thrift shop, pink socks, and heavy shoes with crepe soles. They had shiny faces, angular, heavy profiles, and a look in their eyes that regularly scoured the place for girls. They didn't look at them long, but their dark glance revealed a craving for prey and had a suggestiveness about it that was unmistakable. If the right girl would come along and respond promptly to their aggression with a half smile, they wouldn't hesitate.

Every now and then the plaintive voice of a woman could be heard, and as far as Tom could tell, the story was about a cousin of hers who had developed cancer of the colon and was now heroically facing death.

The diesel buses started up outside with a grunting sound, and their large shadows made their way through the room, across faces, lamps, walls.

This, too, was reality, Tom said to himself. This was stockpiled reality, packed with energy and human destiny. He could see it for this brief moment, and he knew that if he could surrender to this room and devote his life to it, then it would be an abundant and inexhaustible reality to draw on.

He looked at the electric clock. His bus left in ten minutes.

He went outside. He could feel that it was late in the afternoon; the sky was overcast, the fog rose from the river or rolled in from the sea. It was likely to turn quite cold during the night; perhaps there would even be frost after a sunny day like this.

He shuddered.

As the bus pulled up to the platform and the door opened, Tom was anxiously waiting to see if it would be the same driver. Fortunately it wasn't, so he climbed on and paid and sat down in one of the front seats to avoid getting sick once again from the swaying at the rear of the coach.

Just a few women were getting on, and they sat down, chatting away, a couple of seats behind Tom, who nestled in his corner, hoping to close his eyes for a while and perhaps doze off. He explained to himself that he had to win the ten thousand, and nothing in him contradicted that, but he couldn't be bothered to think about it right now. First he had to figure out how to come up with an experience that was true and real.

The thirty kroner made it easier. His heart suddenly felt light, and he decided to buy a couple of steaks, a bag of potato chips, and a bottle of red wine; Etna would probably object, but he would talk her out of it and cheer her up with his bright prospects. Of course, it would be unwise of him to say too much about it, but he couldn't help it; he had to savor the possibility in its brightest glory.

The bus roared on, the thick smell of diesel increased with the heat, and Tom felt a faint nausea. As long as there were no bumps, everything would be fine, because it was not quite time yet for the streets to be turned into giant, crawling larvae or for the brakes to be applied constantly so that the passengers were thrown forward in their seats; the cross streets were almost empty, and even at the larger intersections the traffic lights only throbbed their angry, yellow warnings that meant reduced speed but not the application of brakes with the accompanying sensation of nausea.

They passed the inner suburbs, where the hot dog stands were closing up for the day, and went by the city dump, where sea gulls were hanging like little clouds, billowing up and down, while pieces of dirty paper rose in the air and tumbled across the rubbish heaps and through the stiff grass, where soggy shoes bloomed in the company of rusty cans, broken pottery, and bicycle tires. The dump stretched for miles to the east and west; on the horizon were thick banks of haze, and higher up a thin layer of clouds streamed by. There was a faint turbulence in the air, like a storm coming up when an autumn day has been especially beautiful, before the evening drowns in mist and stillness.

Tom got off the bus one stop before the business district. He spotted a butcher shop immediately to the right, where he was not a regular customer and therefore had no account.

He asked if they had any beef tenderloin, because if they did, he wanted two good slices of it. The butcher was nice, held up the meat so that he could see how good it looked, and cut the steaks according to Tom's directions. That way he would have them exactly the way he wanted them, the butcher said. Tom began patting his pockets and hunting through them.

'You're not going to believe this,' he said to the butcher, who was busily wrapping the meat, 'but I think I forgot my billfold.'

Tom sensed the butcher's composure and friendliness, and he continued, 'Think you could let me charge it? I'll be in first thing in the morning. How early do you open up?'

The butcher smiled broadly and said that that would probably be too early for Tom, because they opened at six in the morning to accommodate the working women who had to get to their jobs and didn't have enough time to do their shopping in the afternoon, but that didn't matter, he could just stop by at his convenience.

Tom gave him his address, took his package, and walked out the door backwards, all the while repeating, 'That was really very kind of you.'

He almost ran down toward the square, momentarily elated at his luck, which made it seem reasonable for him to tell Etna that he had earned twenty-five kroner simply by showing his face and that there was much more to come.

Having reached the square, he went into a grocery store

57

where he hadn't been before either and asked for a bag of potato chips, corrected it to two bags, and asked to see what kind of red wines they had. He held the bottles, put them down on the counter, picked them up again and examined the labels with their pictures of castles and palaces, their names and years, which he didn't know the least thing about; but he had to make a big thing out of it if he wanted to gain credibility. Finally he asked about the prices and chose the third most expensive one, saying that actually it was just as good as the most expensive one. In any case, there was no way of knowing in advance.

He patted his pockets while looking over at the clerk, who was waiting with the items already wrapped in front of him. It wouldn't work, Tom could tell, but he had to give it a try anyway.

'I have a feeling I forgot my money,' Tom said self-consciously. 'It was really dumb of me, but that's the way I am. One of these days I'm going to forget my own self some place or other.'

The clerk didn't seem to register at all. Tom suddenly found his billfold.

'Well, what do you know, here it is after all,' he said cheerfully, shaking his head at his own stupidity.

The clerk pushed the items toward him and said, 'Can you carry it like that?'

'Sure,' Tom said.

He went into the dairy next door and bought butter and a loaf of fresh French bread and a small Camembert, and with bulging pockets and his arms full he headed for home. If Etna was lying on the couch with her back to him, he would dump all the goodies down on her, and although she would get upset, he would find some way of cheering her up, not too much, of course, but enough to make her listen to his account of that fantastic trip, so that she wouldn't interrupt him or make sarcastic remarks or use strong language. Etna actually couldn't be accused of being too cheerful in the first place; but she could have been made happy. Women of her caliber, after all, didn't require too much; for them happiness usually consisted of watching bizarre circus acts or seeing a child beginning to toddle from one chair to another. Ordinary grown-ups were not capable of getting her fired up about anything, but Tom was happy with her at the moment; she had a unique talent for listening, even though she might not understand a whole lot of what he was saying or thought that most of it was nonsense.

Whistling away, he jumped across on the boards in the large puddles in front of his house. He would really have to get hold of a couple of those boards in his neighbor's yard.

He tried the door handle, wanting to push the door open, but it stuck, and he had to use his shoulder, but that didn't do any good either. He knocked on the door and waited. She must have left. He searched through his pockets but couldn't find the key. He jumped up to look in one of the windows, but she wasn't lying in there asleep. He took a couple of turns in front of the stairs until he suddenly felt something heavy against his knee at the bottom of his coat lining. He turned the corner of his coat and carefully manipulated the keys upwards until, with a couple of fingers, he was able to fish them out through the hole in his pocket.

There was a strong smell of kerosene in the house, but the cold had already penetrated, so it must have been a while since she had left for her sister's. Maybe she was making love with somebody in town right now; he couldn't blame her, but it did hurt a little to imagine this, and a jealousy that gnawed at him and sorely wounded his heart made him check the wardrobe to see which dress and shoes she was wearing. He was sure she didn't take money for it. That was really stupid of her; she ought to charge for it, but she couldn't. She was sentimental; she believed, and wanted to believe, that the men did it because they loved her. And then he would have to go and pick her up at her sister's if she didn't come home. But she probably would come home.

He shook the kerosene stove back and forth to find out how

59

much kerosene was left. There wasn't much; he would have to run up to the Bergstrøms' to buy a couple of liters, then he could find out at the same time if they had seen anything of Etna.

The can of Portuguese sardines was still on the primus table, so she had not stayed for lunch. Well, maybe in that case she would be home for dinner. At any rate, he would fix dinner for the two of them and then wait till about seven; otherwise she wouldn't be there, because it turned dark then, and she was afraid of walking alone on the street because of the gardens and all the trees.

If she was not there by seven, she would not come.

Tom emptied all the small items out of his pockets and found the kerosene can, which was rusty and greasy. He always had to wrap the cork in newspaper because no cork apparently existed that fit that kind of can. Disgusting!

On his way to the grocer's Tom was far from in a good mood. He thought about Etna, but mainly about the fact that she hadn't been there when he came home and wanted to surprise her. He had been disappointed. A blind hatred seized him at the thought that she still had enough life and energy in her to pull herself together and go visit her sister or go to a restaurant, where a salesman would wink at her and sit down with her and offer her *smørrebrød* and beer and pay her stupid compliments, dance a few times with her while gazing into her eyes, and then take her to a hotel. Tom muttered this to himself. He had hoped she would be home, for no reason other than that she had to be there so that he wouldn't have to see that she wasn't there but was somewhere else, alive, more alive than he was. He really ought to get rid of her.

He heard the gravel crunching under his feet when he entered the courtyard in front of the Bergstrøms' store, and he suddenly felt that he must get a handle on reality. From this moment on until he left the store he must make it a point to observe everything so that he could portray Mr. and Mrs. Bergstrøm the way they really were.

The doorbell clanged when he walked in. Mrs. Bergstrøm was weighing sugar and didn't speak but glared at him angrily. Bergstrøm was sitting in his office reading the advertising circular that was lying on top of the ledger.

'I'd like three liters of kerosene,' Tom said.

'Bergstrøm,' Mrs. Bergstrøm called.

'I'd like three liters of kerosene,' Tom repeated. 'Hasn't it been nice today?'

'Frankly, we don't have the time to run around and enjoy it,' Mrs. Bergstrøm said.

Bergstrøm took the can.

'Bergstrøm,' the wife said sharply, 'what was it you promised?'

Bergstrøm turned around and looked at Tom.

'I'm not going to let you have anything until you've paid what you owe,' he said.

'Fine with me. I've got money for the kerosene,' Tom said. 'You'll get the rest some other time.'

'Sure we will,' Mrs. Bergstrøm said.

'I'll pay for the kerosene right now,' Tom said, putting ten kroner on the counter.

Mrs. Bergstrøm came closer.

'Where did you get that money?' she said, looking right through Tom.

'From a friend,' Tom said.

'Give him three liters of kerosene,' Mrs. Bergstrom said to her husband. 'We'll keep the rest of the money as a payment toward what he owes.'

'Oh no, you won't,' Tom said.

Mrs. Bergstrøm put the money in the cash register.

'It's for your own sake,' Mrs. Bergstrøm said. 'Otherwise you'll never pay up.'

Tom walked back and forth in front of the counter, muttering to himself: bitch, bitch, bitch, but suddenly he stopped and grabbed a can of tuna in tomato sauce, a package of Swiss cheese triangles, and a can of German wieners.

61

'Then I'd like these items as well,' he said, looking at Mrs. Bergstrøm, who stood with her arms crossed under her chest.

'Well, I'll be . . .' she said slowly. 'Do you want us to call the police?'

'You haven't given me ten kroner's worth,' Tom said. 'It's not for you to decide when I'm supposed to pay what I owe.'

Bergstrøm came back with the kerosene and put the can on the counter.

'He's helping himself,' Mrs. Bergstrøm said. 'Don't give him the kerosene.'

Tom put his hand on a can of tuna.

Bergstrøm looked at his wife and pushed the kerosene can over to Tom.

'We might as well kiss that money goodbye,' Bergstrøm said.

Tom ran down the road, vowing never to set foot in that store again. What did that old biddy think she was doing? He had tolerated her snide remarks long enough, and it was obviously sheer jealousy over the fact that he was not about to piddle his whole life away. He had said goodbye long ago to everything that they believed meant life and happiness and that was finally beginning to do them in. And now they dared to treat him the same way they themselves had been treated!

This was a true, real experience, Tom said to himself. All he had to do was write it down, then the problem would be solved. Nothing could alter the fact that it was real and true, and yet Tom had his doubts. Surely, that wasn't what it was all about. It called for that extra ingredient; it had to have the nature of a vortex that there was no getting away from, not this common, ordinary reality that stretched like tracks of coincidences extending through time, now and then broadening into stations where you could stop for a while and relax a bit.

And yet there was something missing here, maybe the very thing Hiffs wanted him to take pains to experience just once: the reality of physical things, other people's reality. But how? It must be like being mounted in reality, feeling it sitting close and grinding around you, feeling it taking hold of your nerves and your mind, so that a fine rhythm and a stream of tones broke through when you moved a little among all these things that had essence, strength, sound to move you with.

He knew, of course, that all this existed; but what kind of preparation did it take to be able to talk about the experience of a thing? He didn't even dare think of a human being, for that would tear like cogwheels through his flesh. But a thing! Probably even one single thing could be used.

How terrifying to experience the grocer's wife the way she really was, to see those legions of evil spirits lurking behind her unctuous or sarcastic facade, to see her desire in its real dimensions, to see the frayed membranes of her emotional life and the numerous vacant rooms of her brain where a couple of ghosts appeared now and then, pursuing each other and wandering slowly, while moving their hands along the whitewashed walls. And finally, in the depths, to see the cold regent of fear with eyes turned inward, and crooked, clumsy arms struggling to defend himself from quadrangular beings that emerged from the darkness and merely consisted of a jelly-like substance.

Tom shivered. He didn't want to experience that, he couldn't. These needs that people seemed to have, the fact that they wanted each other, that they apparently took up residence in each other, poured life and desire, fear and misery into each other's souls, seemed so terrifying to him that if that was what Hiffs had meant by reality, well, then he didn't want to, and he couldn't. And to hell with the ten thousand.

It was beginning to get dark when he gingerly made his way through the puddles and stood in front of his door and got out the key. Maybe he could go ahead and start dinner so it would be ready when Etna came home, if indeed she did come home.

He fumbled his way inside and put his packages down. He struck a match and lit a candle so that he could see to light the kerosene lamp and the stove. It was a hateful job; he didn't have a funnel, so he missed and got kerosene all over his hands. His whole existence was built on kerosene, he thought; it always smoked and smelled sweetly nauseating, and the air became foul and suffocating with it.

While he was at it, he poured kerosene in the primus as well and began preheating it with alcohol. Then he moved the kerosene stove a little and pushed the lamp back a bit on the table and went over to the window and looked out. It had gotten dark, and the trees stood like charred beings in the fog, which had become dense; there must be thousands of tiny drops on every tree, every trunk, every branch, and maybe they would congeal by some miraculous law and swell, grow heavy, and fall sometime during the night with a reluctant plop.

Etna didn't come. It was too dark. He could go and meet her, because she could have left her sister's house while it was still light, and she could have gotten a late start, and now she would be walking with her heart in her throat, looking around her every step of the way. Tom listened intently for her footsteps; it was as if someone were constantly there, and yet no one came. Every time he gave up, he heard the alcohol hissing in the primus. Finally he stepped outside. It was dripping a little from the roof, and a couple of drops fell on his head, but below the stairs they couldn't reach him. Without thinking, he felt his way across the boards and got out to the road, where he stood until he began to get cold; then he quickly fled inside.

The primus had gone out. He tried pumping it and letting in the kerosene, but it burned red and sooty; he would have to start all over. He filled it with alcohol again, lit it, and walked around the room, keeping an eye on the alcohol flame. It always took too long, but finally the flame went out, and he had to pump the stove and pull a match out of the box almost at the same time, but the match broke; luckily he got it on the next try, and the primus sputtered and sizzled with a blue flame.

He took out the frying pan, put it on the fire, and opened the package of meat so that it would be ready when the pan reached the right temperature. Then he uncorked the red wine and helped himself to a glass. With his hand close to the bottom of the skillet, he checked to see if it was hot enough and then put the meat on.

A few minutes later, the steaks were done, and he turned off the primus, put the pan over on the table, and took out two glasses and two plates and knives and forks, arranging the packages of butter and Camembert and potato chips and fresh French bread so that they would look nice on the table.

Etna didn't come. She was probably crying her heart out at her sister's. Her sister was divorced and the mother of two small children, and she was a monster of protectiveness and always tried to get Etna riled up; Etna could easily find another man, she said. Her sister always knew lots of men who wanted to get married; *she* didn't want to marry them, but they would be fine for Etna, and those were probably the men they went out with in the evening, when he was told they had gone to a movie, and that way Etna had gotten on the wrong track and was probably starting to get ideas of her own. He had never caught her at anything, he was simply guessing, and it didn't matter anyway; they were just thoughts that came and went without making any major impression on him. But this particular evening she ought to have been home.

Tom lit a cigarette and went out on the steps. It was only twenty after seven; she might still come home. He would wait five minutes. Somewhere in the fog he heard voices, the deep voice of a man and the high voice of a woman, billowing toward each other about some banal subject. The voices trailed off, and Tom now heard the nervous hammering of the two-stroke engines just before and after the traffic circle and the droning roar of a large car as it sped out of town.

He threw his cigarette in the nearest puddle and went inside. The steaks had already turned dull and were probably cold by now. He had no appetite but sat down anyway and cut off a chunk of the meat and ate it and then another one, poured himself a glass of red wine and downed it in one draft, poured himself another glass and drank it, too. But there was no real enjoyment in it; he might as well have eaten a liverwurst or salami sandwich.

He was alone, and he noticed that things were against him, his house was against him, the silence was against him, whenever he wasn't doing anything. Fear lay like a ring around his heart. He wasn't afraid of anything, he didn't believe in ghosts, and who would murder him, anyway, but there was a fear whose hour belonged to loneliness, idleness; in it, emptiness sprouted needles and thorns, and he had to suffer for a long time until lassitude finally came to soothe him. He considered going to pick Etna up, then he would have her to flee from, but he didn't have the energy; besides, he had probably better start writing, that is, if he was able to. It would be easy to write his novel now, he thought: he could write about Mrs. Bergstrøm's secret life, about people's secret lives, but it would never be as real as Hiffs wanted, because Hiffs would probably think it was all imagination, all guesswork on his part. Hiffs wanted something else; he would have to work hard to get at irrefutable reality.

He knew, of course, that he was born and had been confirmed, that he had parents, had gone to school and passed his exams with a grade of B-, that he barely weighed 135 lbs., that train tickets within the city were yellow, and that the present government was social-liberal; he knew that man was descended from the ape and the ape from the amoeba, and that God was a free invention, which man had plagued himself with for a couple of thousand years, according to psychoanalysis and other well-meaning movements; he knew that the forest at times was green and the sky blue and that these were mere optical truths; he knew there were poor people and rich people and that it didn't have to be that way if only communism could be introduced. These were givens, although that might not always have been the case. But reality it was not.

Tom picked up his fork, pressed it hard, and mumbled that this was reality; sure it was reality, but he really couldn't care less. Even if he went blind staring at the fork for hours, even if he went into ecstasy and experienced the whole essence of that fork, it would amount at best to fascinating humbug, but never to reality. Maybe for Hiffs or others who had this ability to live in the present wherever they were, for whom life opened and closed like juicy, nourishing spaces.

And what was a landscape or a face other than a jarring image hovering before his eyes and burning to cinders before he had time to take it in? The outside world was like remnants of glimpses, and he wouldn't be able to say with certainty whether or not it existed. Well, it probably did exist whenever you needed it for your own purposes, then it would be of immeasurable importance and inviolable value, but you could avoid it more or less. Wasn't reality rather what you couldn't avoid, what couldn't be explained away? Everything could be explained away, but not reality, it had to remain fixed. That was what Hiffs had meant.

Tom got up and paced the floor a few times; he was vaguely conscious of existence with its incohesiveness and sadness, like a forest that is slowly rotting away and collapsing with bark and fungi and beetles along a river that doesn't know where it's coming from, doesn't know where it's going.

He could write about that, he said to himself, and he hurried into the other room to get the typewriter and the paper.

6.

Acrid air wafted toward him when he opened the door to the little room. The yellowish light from the kerosene lamp followed him as he walked in. He pushed the chair in under the table and groped for the typewriter, but he couldn't reach it. Etna must have put it on the floor. He felt his way around to one side of the table and then the other, in between the table legs and underneath the table, ran his hand over the plush cover of the couch, and got down on his hands and knees and put one hand in under the couch and slid it over the floorboards, which were rough and full of splinters. He felt his way along the baseboard all around the room and went out to get the lamp, which sent up a thin streak of soot as he carried it in. He looked around the room. The typewriter wasn't there.

He shook his head in disbelief and went into the other room, put the lamp down on the dining room table, opened the wardrobe, and rummaged among dresses, which smelled of mildew and Etna's sweat, and shoes, whose leather was stiff and smelled like a bog. He grabbed a chair and checked the top of the wardrobe, where the old weeklies lay in disorderly piles; he struck a match and looked under the wardrobe where the floor was thick with dust. The typewriter wasn't there.

Tom didn't understand. He moved the couch and the chairs, opened the dresser drawers, and finally went outside to check the outhouse, but the typewriter wasn't there. Etna must have taken it. She had probably sold it to a second-hand shop for peanuts, and now she was squandering the money along with her lover, probably some seedy fellow who could make her do whatever he wanted her to by begging and pleading with her, and she was soft, she wanted to mother him and help him, and then she had taken the typewriter; unless, of course, it had been revenge on her part, because she had been upset, after all, and then you never knew what she might do. She became blind with rage and didn't know what she was doing; all she could think of was retaliating one way or another. Maybe she hadn't even sold it but had thrown it into someone's yard or down into the excavation for their house so that he would see it. That way they would be sure to have an argument, which for a few minutes at least would keep his attention focused on her. She felt so mistreated from not being used, from not being seen or heard or addressed. Because that's the way it was, he knew that, but he couldn't do anything about it. Maybe she had had enough of him.

Tom didn't feel the least bit bitter toward her right now. She was gone, but maybe she'd be back some day and would sit in the wicker chair and smoke cigarettes, if he didn't go and pick her up before long. In two days, in three days, when he would bring her one krone's worth of carnations, she would push him aside when he came close and told her all those things he didn't mean and yet did mean, but she would go along, and she would stay with him for a while until something else happened or something flared up in her so that she would be tempted to go out with the salesmen again. But he was nevertheless her destiny. Otherwise she wouldn't have taken the typewriter.

He thought about what Hiffs had said about him. It was true, but he didn't feel it. They said that the truth hurt, but it didn't hurt him, not even now that his life was open to scrutiny without his having anything to say about it. He was proud, Hiffs had said, that was true, and he remained proud because what he felt like most right now was smiling, the only way he knew how: grimacing.

The phrases he had used about the forest that was rotting away and the river were too elegant; he didn't have anything against expressing things so they sounded good, but it was too elegant for Hiffs' taste, he had to be more sober. But what good would that do now that he was without a typewriter. He couldn't write with a pencil, because there was something about a pencil that demanded more seriousness or formality than he could muster; he became paralyzed with fear whenever he had a pencil in his hand.

Tom paced the floor and muttered to himself without knowing what he was saying; he simply had to generate movement now that he couldn't get anything written. But loneliness closed in on him from all sides, like narrowness and like cold, and he suddenly longed for something and thought that that was reality, the fact that he was actually longing for something, and he took the alarm clock, which was sitting on the dresser, and wound it and felt the resistance of the spring and its tightness when it was wound up all the way, and he looked at the indifferent circle of numbers on the dial, at the name of the company, and felt the cool surface, which told him nothing and never would tell him anything. But the clock was ticking loudly and audibly now. He took a round ceramic vase from a shelf above the dresser, and its form was spherical, and the resistance from inside pressed against his hand, but it remained just an empty vase with long, dry stalks of silver dollars that rattled when he blew on them. They had been there a year, and they had often talked about throwing them out, but they never did.

It was as if he had to try to fill himself one last time, and he went out into the yard and sank into the heavy, clayey ground. And the trees were around him; they were living beings that were asleep now, although they were alive in their sleep, and they stretched from their roots in the dark unconsciousness of the earth up to the black, gnarled branches that received the light and the wind. He put his hand on one of the low, wet branches, which was slimy with lichen; he tried to grip the thin trunk of the tree with both hands. He couldn't do it, but it didn't matter, because now he knew what he wanted to know, that the trees do not speak with a human voice, they answer only with flowers and fruit; they do not lie down in our arms, they fall only at the blade of the ax, and they yearn for no one.

Maybe he missed Etna, maybe she was the only thing he did miss, and the other things had only pointed the way to this one being, who could meet him and speak and envelop him; but this he could not experience because the strength left his body when the time came, a panic arose in all his thoughts, all his feelings, all the parts of his body, and he felt that now he was being annihilated, now he was committing himself to fire, now he would never write that novel.

He couldn't, he didn't want to, and he had no faith in himself either.

And yet, maybe reality was to meet another human being and to merge with that person, like waves that are unaware whether they are alone or together but fill each other with strength, that crest and fall and are enriched by each other's being. He had to laugh as he finished this thought, he felt like running, because what would Hiffs say when he came across a couple of sentences about how he missed his wife. After all, he didn't miss his wife, he didn't give a hoot about her, she could go jump in the lake for all he cared, with all her traveling salesmen. He could take care of himself. He would have peace and quiet to write his novel when she was gone, and when it was published, she would be sorry that she hadn't stayed with him and enjoyed her share of the fame; but that was her business.

He slowly went inside and thought about how stupid he had acted. All his emotions were gathered in his hands, they had gotten heavier with them, and he couldn't get rid of them. It was sheer hysteria, but it wasn't the first time; he had done it three times before when he was alone. And all those years in his youth when he still nourished some faint hope, and when he had leaned against walls, which were still warm from the day, and had seen people hurrying by and thought that one person would break away from the crowd and come to him. That had never happened.

He had barely gone inside before it occurred to him that

there would probably never be a better night to go get the boards than this one, and he went out again, staggering over the puddles and slowly sauntering into his neighbor's yard, where the boards lay neatly stacked. They were long, heavy, fresh; he took three of them, although he needed only two, and carried them in his arms as if they were pieces of firewood and threw them over in front of the door to the outhouse and placed some cardboard boxes and rusty sheet metal over them so that his neighbor wouldn't notice them in case he missed them and came looking for them in a day or two.

He didn't believe in reality, he said to himself as he paced the floor again and hunted in his pockets for a cigarette, because what did it mean to have a real, true experience when five minutes later you didn't have the energy to believe in it anymore? Wasn't reality like a big, heavy burden, a rock of Atlas that was placed on your shoulders and that you couldn't ever unload without the world and your own life collapsing? But that kind of reality he wasn't familiar with. And who was, anyway? Wasn't life for most people like a ride on an underground train that suddenly goes through open, lighted shafts, where one's consciousness is filled, only to move on into these dark, monotonous tunnels where nothing is and can be?

The world could be proven, but most of it was void of consciousness and therefore without reality. Nature was alive, that could be proven and felt and seen and heard, but its reality wasn't good for much of anything, it was destroyed in an instant after a few predictable seconds. And that's the way it was with human beings: they disappeared from view the instant they appeared, and this longing he had sensed for a moment went away just like love affairs go away, like sorrows, pain, enjoyment, all those emotions that make their triumphant entrance into one's mind and eventually die. At least they did in him. He knew of nothing that had really lasted in his mind other than this brief light that was followed by the long darkness, these feeble little thrusts of the will that collapsed under the tombstones of lassitude and now formed endless cemeteries, letting him know in no uncertain terms how little he had accomplished.

Hiffs had been able to maintain a reality with his will; he had been able to work with himself in large, open spaces, he had this firm yet pliable structure in his mind that could branch out and still remain itself; he had this rhythm within him that seemed to be not just an appreciation of life as such but of the certainty of reality as well. This was the secret that Hiffs couldn't reveal and that it would be unwise for others to copy, since there was no salvation from the dissolution that characterized himself. For this secret, which consisted in being receptive, not by becoming just one large ear or one large eye, but in being receptive with one's whole being so that the simple things became deep and the deep straightforward, so that it seemed that it was the meaning of the world and of reality that was given consciousness here – this was the dividing line here on earth that separated human beings into two categories, the one including many, the other kind only few.

For him, reality was a tiny, accurate characterization of himself, because he had never had the energy to experience anything else, as most people don't. He could, of course, name all these acute glimpses of the exterior world where some contact was made that overpowered the moment, but these experiences and these emotions never became that nourishment which made the tree grow again, so that a great, free reality developed where the 'I' roamed in the avenues of late summer, near voices, bodies, only to return to the cool plazas of thought.

The only thing that was reality to him, permissible reality, paid-for reality, was a few brutal sentences that told the truth about himself the way he avoided hearing it but the way it nevertheless resounded so persistently through the labyrinth of his unconsciousness and through the deplorable din of trivial events. It would never have occurred to him to write them down if Hiffs hadn't been crazy enough to offer him ten thousand for rendering a real, true experience. Maybe there were other things that made up the truth about him, some here and some there, but these couldn't be included now, because they could be contradicted, they would need time to take hold, and that probably wouldn't happen, so he had no right to call them his own.

Tom sat down at the table and tasted the cold meat and drank some of the red wine, certain that he could come up with the three or four sentences that would be sufficient. He could try to find them before morning, but he could also put off the job till the next day. He drank one glass after the other, he was overcome with drowsiness, and, he thought now and then, it would be a good idea to go to bed so that he would be fresh in the morning. But he remained sitting there anyway, drinking absentmindedly, and when there was nothing left in the bottle, he let sleep overpower him and slept like that until his feet got cold. Then he got up, pulled the bedding out of the drawer under the couch, kicked off his shoes, took off his coat, and crawled under the quilts.

But sleep refused to come. A stubborn alertness had seized control of his nerves, and he lay there for the longest time, swearing at the lamp, which he didn't feel like turning off, at the damp sheet, which made him sweat and freeze at the same time, and at the tightening dryness in his mouth, which always came after drinking red wine and which there was no getting rid of. He snorted at those feelings of repression that struggled out of his subconscious, weighing him down so that he knew he wouldn't be allowed to fall asleep immediately.

He pressed his head into his pillow, trying to lie on one side and then the other, while attempting to let his thoughts gently nudge him toward sleep, but now there were many of them, like flies buzzing out from their hiding places, and he was finally stretched to the breaking point and had to jump out of bed and put on his shoes and pace the floor, and it was freezing cold in the room. The kerosene was burned up, and if he used the rest of the can during the night, there wouldn't be any left by morning when he had to write and it would be more important than ever to have some heat.

Nevertheless, he poured out the rest of the kerosene and lit the stove, squatting next to it to warm himself. He was wide awake and thought he might as well write now as later. It couldn't take too long. Sure, he didn't have his typewriter, but he could print the letters on the paper with his pencil, then it would be easier, because he couldn't stand writing them out longhand, he always felt he was on the verge of getting tendinitis in his wrist as soon as he had written two lines.

He removed the plates, serving dishes, and glasses from the table and went and got a piece of paper and a pencil from the other room; it got spots on it right away from the little red lakes of wine, but that didn't matter, that way the circumstances would leave their mark on everything, it was just fine that way. He sat there holding on to his pencil, putting it down and picking it up and putting it down again, because now the only thing he needed was to smoke a cigarette, then he would be able to write, and then that business would be settled.

He searched his pockets unsystematically, but when he was done, he was sure he didn't have another butt left. He put on his coat and checked to see that he had money, banged the door shut behind him, made it across the boards, and got out to the road, where there was a strong smell of the fields on the other side through the fog. Gardens had their smell, fields had theirs, houses had theirs, people had theirs. Even fog smelled like the places it came from; this one was a local suburban fog. Eventually, he reached the first intersection where a lamp was hanging high above, looking at him with its face of light, which spread out concentrically into the fog, and he moved through this new quality that the fog had and then back into the darkness, then into the light, and so on from light to dark, from dark to light, without seeing the houses and the hedges of the gardens until he reached the Bergstrøms', where the fluorescent lights by the gas pumps were on all night, and where you could glimpse the facades of the houses on both sides of the road with their massive, dense blackness.

The light was on upstairs at the Bergstrøms', and Tom imagined how Mrs. Bergstrøm was sitting there counting money and how she would be startled now when she heard the crunch of the gravel, how the blind would be raised carefully and the two faces would peer out; actually, he ought to stand down there and laugh at them, but he didn't feel up to it. He took two single kroner out of his pocket and walked over to the automat as quietly as he could, found the brand he wanted, put his money in, and pulled out the drawer. When he had taken the pack, he tried squeezing his fingers in to reach the next pack, because maybe then he could tear it open and help himself to a couple of cigarettes from that one, but it was impossible. He stole away as close to the wall as possible and felt he had made it when he finally stood on the other side of the road and tore the pack open and lit up. At long intervals, a car would come down the highway, its yellow cones of light groping their way along the pavement as if they had lost something.

Tom trudged down the road and decided to make tea when he got home. That would warm him up and stimulate him so that he could sit and enjoy himself while writing the three or four lines, which he would have to get done so that he could go and see Hiffs first thing in the morning. He got the primus lit and walked through the house whistling until the water boiled, so that he had to hurry to get the teapot and the loose tea and pour the water before it had boiled away.

Now the time had come. He put the teapot on a plate and placed a cup next to it, took the paper and the pencil, and carefully doodled in a corner of the paper to test the pencil, and then he wrote in light, elongated letters:

> My eyes are blind,
> my hands are withered,
> my soul is afflicted with annihilation.

That's the way it was, he didn't know anything else. He had gotten a little poem out of it, but he hadn't intended to; it wasn't too much, it wasn't too little, it was just right. He wrote above it: 'My Reality' and had to laugh when he thought how little space it took up and how amusing it was that this little scrap of paper

76

would bring in ten thousand, that is, if Hiffs wasn't pulling his leg.

He poured himself a cup of tea and gulped it down; then he got the idea that maybe he ought to add a sentence in parentheses so that nothing would be left out. He added: 'I'm writing this to earn ten thousand,' then all his wretchedness had been included, and Hiffs couldn't demand anything more of him.

He drank one cup of tea after the other, and it turned bitter, and finally it began to make him sick, and he just sat and smoked, enjoying the fact that he had accomplished something, and it was as if it were ten thousand miles behind him, it was true and yet it wasn't true, because at this realization he had conquered new possibilities that he couldn't see clearly yet, but in his relief he interpreted them to be promising, his life would be brighter and more coherent. Maybe it was possible to get closer to reality in some other way, to get out of himself, out to the beach near the ocean. He believed it for these few minutes, and he grew in his own eyes, became fresher and freer, and he didn't mind, he had mouldered long enough in life's corner.

He thought about Etna, who was walking around so uptight and totally unable to cope, she was so defenseless and helpless. He felt so strong right now, he would know how to cheer her up any number of ways now that they would have money, and even if they couldn't have a child of their own, they could adopt one, and it would mean quite a bit to him, too, that Etna was busy with the child and everything connected with it. He would have more strength if he didn't always have to have Etna underfoot, he would be himself, he would be able to write. If he could. Because now he had a scrap of paper in front of him that he knew by heart and that would repeat itself inside him whenever he started a project, and every line he would write must have that quality about it, there would be no way around it, and how many lines of that sort could you actually write the rest of your life? He had struck a bargain – not with the Devil but with another Mightier One, who was forcing him to name his own terms, which he could adhere to later on only by being silent and saying nothing.

He didn't want to believe that, it couldn't be that exacting. When all was said and done, he did have talent and could write, shouldn't he then use that talent? Well, he could do his best, his utmost, but he knew it wouldn't be any use. It would be vanity versus reality, vanity versus everything that lived and sang or moaned right in the world's heart, in life's heart, and that waited patiently for the hour of strength before moving toward the center; it didn't roam in the uncertain, the exterior, the impatient; it preferred to reside in the mundane everyday, which is where humans wait and prepare for that ultimate awareness.

He could write only two or three lines more if he didn't want to write against himself, because this runaway imagination of his, which he had always been so proud of, couldn't hold a candle to the fir tree, the snail's house, or to the sun's course through the ecliptic, because those things *existed*; fantasy existed only in the most mediocre entertainment. And what good did it do that he knew all about Mrs. Bergstrøm and her husband and their avarice? It wouldn't be any more of a reality to write about them, because he didn't really have what it took, it would only turn to dross and drivel. He knew how to write deliberate untruths, he knew how to write lies, he could make an effort to conquer the lies, but they would be there, there was no getting rid of them. He had no intention of being that consistent.

Tom realized that he could go to sleep now, and he kicked off his shoes and threw his topcoat and his sports coat on a chair and crawled under the quilts. He lay there for a while, enjoying his rest. He relaxed completely and let sleep rise through the nooks and crannies of his consciousness; he was lifted, sucked into the aqueous trembling, and he felt dreams take shape far away, deep down, while drifting through this ocean which didn't have the one-sided direction of energy that being awake did and that therefore carried him everywhere and let everything that arose retain its shape through some incomprehensible grace. This was where he wanted to be now.

7.

'Now I'm being cast out into the world,' Tom thought, when he reluctantly opened his eyes and glimpsed the gray, cautious light of morning in his room, and now he had to embark on that strenuous process that each new day demanded of him, where you ran and ran only to get nowhere. He did have reason to get up today, but then you could always dream up some reason to get out of bed, although it was rarely a very cheerful one. He must get those lines to Hiffs, and he would get his money, and then he would go into town in the evening and pick up Etna and take her to a movie and out to eat afterwards. He wasn't going to hold it against her at all that she had taken the typewriter. He understood; he wanted her to have a new coat, and they would talk about the house, or maybe it would be an even better idea to move out to the country and live in a farmhouse.

He had dreamed about turtles during the night: ten turtles were sitting on top of each other, and every time the one on the bottom struggled forward a little, the nine on top had difficulty keeping their balance on the domed shell. They stretched out their legs as far as they could, trying to hold on to the one below, but the stack rocked back and forth, and he was afraid they would fall off and break their shells, and it was impossible to figure out how they would ever get off each other's back.

Maybe it was because he had found a pond turtle in the garden one fall, and he had brought it inside, and Etna liked it so much she would feed it and let it bite her finger, and he had begun to get jealous and said that it smelled, and, when that didn't do any good, that it belonged to one of the neighbors, so they had to return it, but Etna didn't want to give it up. Then he had taken it one day, when she was visiting her sister, and put it in a garden down the road, but when Etna came home and didn't find it, she was unhappy, and since that time things had been worse with her than ever. He had tried to buy her a new turtle, but she didn't want it. Maybe this had some connection with the typewriter, for it was entirely possible that Etna had taken the typewriter because he had taken the turtle away from her. She had called the turtle Amo, the only word she knew in Latin.

Dreams were so real while you were dreaming them, they rarely contradicted themselves, and although you might dream crazy things sometimes, there was something powerful about them that the state of being awake never had. But he hardly ever dreamed, less and less nowadays. Most nights were uneventful like his days; more and more, he was aware of the sharp transitions.

He pushed the quilts aside and swung his legs over the edge of the bed, where he sat for a while getting his bearings and looking out in the garden where the air was clear as silver in the light haze. He got up, unfastened his belt, and tucked his shirt in and brushed his pants up and down with his hands so that the wrinkles wouldn't be so noticeable, and he put on his shoes, which felt wet and cold. He remembered that Etna had accused him of not washing properly, so he splashed some water into the basin and rubbed his face over and over again till he felt refreshed. He ought to shave too, but he had used his only blade many times; it tore his skin. There was no point in going to pick up Etna with a face full of little cuts; she would be ashamed in front of her sister, who never minded going on at length about how bad he looked, even right to his face. She was the one who had taught Etna that kind of thing.

He went outside to answer a call of nature behind the house and accidentally did it on the cardboard and the sheet metal that covered the three boards, which he wouldn't be able to put in their proper places right away now, even though it would look nice and Etna would be pleased when she had to make her way across the puddles at night. He also ought to remove that spade, but the soil was especially soft right where the spade was, so that had better wait, although that too would please Etna. She wanted a bit of garden to care for, and he had promised her many times that he would dig it, but he hadn't gotten around to it, because every time he had dug a few shovelfuls, he felt the urge to write, and that took precedence over everything else, and although he hadn't gotten started anyway, he had stopped digging, because just maybe he would be able to write, but not if he had to dig now. Of course, Etna could have done the digging herself, but she lost her enthusiasm when he didn't show any; then it was no fun, she said. You had to have your heart in it, and he had told her so often that his heart was in it all right, only not just now, but she wanted to do it only right this minute; if they waited, she saw no point in it. And actually, neither did he.

For that reason they never had flowers, other than the ones that cropped up in the garden by themselves, and which he had tried in vain to make Etna see were much more beautiful than the ones you cultivated. She didn't care for them, because to her they amounted to carelessness and disorder in a garden where their own flowers were meant to grow; the fact that they existed in the first place was a real shame, because, as he admitted, they had plenty of time, but she never pulled herself together, she lacked motivation. If she could have kept her turtle, maybe she would have taken care of the garden herself.

Gardens were one of the first subjects they had discussed when they met. It was one evening when he was at one of those run-down dinner restaurants where all the tablecloths were covered with gravy spots and the waiters barely had time to clear a table before a new crowd was heading for the vacant seats and the chance to get a plateful of beef stew with brown gravy and mounds of boiled potatoes for 2.35. The place was permeated with the smell of food, the smell of a dish that was a mishmash of every imaginable leftover, and the temperature of

81

the room was kept too high so that you felt dizzy from the moment you entered. He had found only one empty seat and had taken it, and there across from him was Etna. He didn't notice her but ensconced himself behind his newspaper until the waiter came and took his order and he asked for beef stew like the rest. Then he happened to notice Etna, who was just sinking her teeth into some pastry, while looking up at the waiter and then around the room at all the men who were sitting there drinking light beer or seltzer. Every time a man looked at her she would smile, and Tom thought right away that she was a little too encouraging, until she looked at him and smiled and he realized that it was simply naiveté and loneliness that had not yet turned to despair.

He had glanced in her direction several times, and every time she hit it lucky, as she just happened to be looking in his direction and smiling; he quickly hid behind his newspaper, and behind it he could hear the waiter treating her with condescension and making cracks when she ordered more pastry. She loved pastry, he had learned later.

He had eaten slowly behind his paper, but he stayed on, nevertheless, as the restaurant emptied out and people hurried off to a movie, back to the office, to visit friends, or to look for a prostitute. As he turned the pages, he saw her now and then sitting with her cup halfway between her mouth and the saucer, staring at him. He had been kind of frightened. Finally, he had scanned the entertainment section, and he heard her getting up and saying 'Bye,' and he lowered his paper and said 'Bye' and got up and followed her to the corner where the coats were hanging; he helped her on with her coat, and she said thanks. Then they had gone to a movie, and he hadn't been able to shake her. Fate, they called it.

He went inside and poured alcohol in the primus to preheat it, and while the flame was burning down, he leafed through the story magazines and the weeklies that Etna brought home with her from her sister's, who got them from another woman, who got them for free because her daughter was a receptionist in a dentist's office, where they got a new supply of magazines every couple of weeks. The stories in them were inane, but they got into print somehow, and he had not been able to figure out how to write that sort of thing himself, because everything he had ever submitted had come right back. He probably didn't write poorly enough for them.

The preheating was almost over; he got the primus going and put the kettle on, straightened up the counters, and stacked the dirty dishes so that things would look nice when Etna came home, and when the water boiled, he poured water on the tea leaves from the night before and then added some fresh ones. It tasted terrible, but it was hot, and that was the main thing. He also grabbed a couple of slices of French bread and smeared some butter on them and ate them to soften the blow of the tea.

When he had lit a cigarette, he put on his coat and left. Just as he was locking up, he felt something behind him, and when he turned around, he noticed the neighbor's black dog coming toward him with its tail wagging happily, but when he instinctively reached out to pet it, it panicked, jumped back, and took off down through the garden, disappearing through the hole in the hedge where it usually showed up every day around this time before coming up to the window to watch him while he worked.

He walked briskly down the road, patting the inner pocket of his overcoat a few times to see if he had the scrap of paper with the lines on it, which he simply mustn't lose, but it was there. He reached the wide road, where the brick apartment complexes loomed in the fog with their large glass surfaces, balconies, and French doors, and on the lawns between the buildings men were raking up the last brown leaves from the small trees that struggled there. Tom hurried past the butcher shop, his coat up around his ears, and almost tripped over a wagon with eight kindergarten kids in it.

The bus was just disappearing from view on its way toward town when he reached the bus stop, and he paced back and forth by the stanchion, jittery at the thought of having to spend twenty minutes in a place that seemed so unreasonably deserted if you didn't have the money to make a haul at the stores. He looked at the trucks and the refrigerated vans passing through the traffic circle from the north, and at the milk trucks in front of the two dairies, but in the long run he couldn't watch them, they made him sick. When he checked again to see exactly what time the bus would arrive, he discovered that the bus ran only twice an hour and that it would be thirty minutes now until the next one came. But there was another bus that took a longer route before ending its rounds near a station where he could catch a train that would take him out to Hiffs. He didn't notice this until the bus pulled up to the sidewalk and opened its door.

Tom got on and eagerly took a handful of coins from his coat pocket while asking if the bus connected with a train for the towns along the coast, and the driver was good enough to check his schedule, which indicated that there was only a twenty-minute wait at the station; unfortunately, it was a slow train that stopped at any station where passengers had to get on and off. Tom felt much better now and sat down right behind the driver and asked how long the train would take to get to the beach; the driver told him approximately, one more passenger got on, then the driver looked at his watch, released the hand brake, clutched, put the bus in gear, and clutched again so gently that Tom didn't feel the bus was already moving. He was elated and told the driver that he must have a special touch when it came to using the clutch, it was just like touching the cheek of a child, because he had never experienced anything like it. As a rule, he would get sick as soon as the bus started moving. One driver in particular, who had the route into town, was simply atrocious.

The driver smiled indulgently. Tom leaned back in his seat and enjoyed the ride and the fresh air that was streaming in through a little sliding window.

They followed the wide beltway for a while, then they turned off on a narrow secondary road where the elms were dripping with fog and where men and women in dark clothes occasionally would raise a hand, and the bus had to stop, and they got

84

aboard with their pungent smell of weather and fields and animals. The bus was filled with conversation between people who were speaking slowly and calmly; it seemed to Tom that they still hadn't realized that the city had gotten frightfully close to their fields and farms.

The fog quietly melted away, and you could see far out over the fields where the tractors were moving about with their manure spreaders, plows, and harrows, and where lovely old trees were standing, which no one had had the heart to cut down yet though they were actually in the way. They went through villages, stopping for a few minutes outside a bakery or a grocery to drop off or take on packages, and occasionally a girl would knock on the window and talk to someone on the bus, and their breath would make a blue patch on the pane. They passed the radial roads from the city, where they had to stop until there was a break in the traffic, and again and again they came across areas covered with garden plots where the sun-flowers lay broken now and the beans were turning brown on their stalks, or they passed small clusters of one-story houses where the yards were full of laundry and the women were digging up potatoes and piling them into tin pans, while weathervanes in the shape of airplanes perched on mounds of flintstones and green glass balls.

The people who got on in these places were rugged and stubborn-looking; they were pale from drudgery, lean and shabbily dressed, and had the obstinate, watchful glance of the loner, and the women who came with one or two kids, whom they had on their laps and at their knees, had faces with dreams written on them that they clung to and suffered from because they could never be fulfilled, and Tom felt how they were surrounded by the chilling scorn of the farmers, because they owned almost nothing, they only coveted, but they were the last to wish to accomplish anything themselves – and they had to pay for that.

From the low, far-reaching hills that the road followed here and there, you could see the city with its suburbs, and the farmers looked toward town, nodding and saying to each other, 'The fog is lifting, it's going to be a nice day' – and the space grew upwards, the blue peeked through the breaks in the clouds, and toward the east over the pine forests it was like a shower of light falling, and in the midst of it a cluster of farms was clearly visible.

'Yes, it's almost like spring,' Tom heard them saying.

Before the bus pulled into the town where the train station was, most people had gotten off and disappeared into houses and farms with women, men, or children who had come to meet them, and except for Tom there were only two people left on the bus. They looked as if they might be businessmen, and they too wanted to catch the train.

Tom went into the waiting room and had to settle for a one-way ticket, because he had almost no money left, but he allowed himself one glass of anisette at the bar, which was ruled by a fat meathead, who leaned over the counter and had a real knack for picking up a glass and a bottle with one hand to avoid getting up. He didn't say anything, but his watchfulness nevertheless monitored every word the porters and the extra staff laughingly confided to each other, as they ate hard rolls piled with meat and drank apple brandy out of small pointed glasses. The businessmen were standing at the opposite wall in front of the pinball machines, smoking fat cigars and looking straight ahead under their black velvet hats.

A train full of lumber was just pulling in slowly and was switched onto the sidetrack, and the porters immediately started discussing the price of lumber, which was rising steadily so that it was practically impossible anymore to build houses made out of wood; the lumber barons were getting fatter and fatter, although the forests ought to belong to everyone so that no one would have an advantage. Yes, one person asserted, certainly the barons of old owned the rights to the land, but the trees after all grew up in the air, and they hadn't bought that, so everything in the air surely must belong to the state.

They roared with laughter while Tom stood and mused over

this magnificent display of merriment that apparently could go on all day or might go on for most of their lives, because this station surely was overstaffed, they all had plenty of time to chat. Only it was puzzling how these people who didn't do anything and never went anywhere except to this place could continue to have something to talk about. Did a five-minute experience give them enough for five hours worth of chatter? A run-in with the traffic assistant, a passenger with a big red nose, a girl you could have seduced if you had felt like it. These were stock characters who kept on performing their drama, which consisted in developing all those combinations that evolved of their own accord and never stopped evolving. Each one was a stock character, Tom noticed, and the others he worked hard at making into stock characters. Although all of them were demonstrably right here in this place and got paid for it to boot, each one had his heroic or comic specialty, which they all mutually agreed to believe was the other person's ineradicable need or weakness. You didn't notice you were here, you constantly followed the scene and witnessed in turn one person loving twelve girls in two hours, the next beating three wealthy farmers at cards and winning 2000 kroner in one evening, the third getting locked up by his wife as soon as he came home, the fourth being served his favorite dish by his mother every day. The only person who knew he was here was the meathead; he had nothing to say, but he took their money.

The train steamed into the station; a couple of porters put their glasses down on the counter and walked out, the two businessmen and Tom close behind. There were three passenger cars and a combination freight and mail car, from which the conductor was already throwing sacks of mail out onto the platform.

Tom climbed up on the front platform of the second passenger car and stayed there when the train started up with a jerk and moved out through the fields, brown and newly plowed or still green, which stretched all the way down toward the wet meadows near the mouth of the river, where you could almost make out the endless row of high poplars along its bank. There was a strong smell on the platform; the coal dust from the engine swirled down so that Tom got specks of dust in his eyes and had to rub them till the tears streamed down his face. A few kilometers before they reached the wooded area, they went through a wide belt of tall yellow grass, and here a gust of wind swept away the last layer of fog, and the light broke through in a wave that sailed through the grass, chasing dark shadows ahead of it.

The sun shone bright between the trunks of tall mountain firs where the workers were cutting long slits in the bark and placing small zinc cups that would be full of resin in about a week and that other workers would empty into tall containers which they carried on their backs. At other places in the forest they were cutting down trees, and hefty workhorses were pulling the logs out to the roads, from where they were transported to the fragrant mill towns in the narrow clearings with their red-painted sawbarns and yellow mountains of sawdust and stacks of freshly cut boards and laths. Here the train made frequent whistle-stops where someone would get off or on, and Tom heard the sounds of the buzz saws and wood thrown on top of wood. He thought about the fact that he had never been here before, although it was fairly close to town; he hadn't been to the coast either, and he hadn't made one single excursion to make Etna happy. It had seemed impossible to him; if he had even considered it, he didn't quite remember. And who knew if it was really that uplifting to walk through these green and red corridors once you were there and everything looked the same, so that you inevitably would get lost once evening arrived. He had never really cared for nature. He occasionally noticed it was there; it amazed him that anything actually existed other than himself. But he couldn't imagine moving out to the woods; it probably wasn't any better there than elsewhere. But for Hiffs it seemed to have something to offer.

He felt a certain pleasure in being led through this colorful countryside, but it didn't take hold of him, nothing could happen to him, and how could anything actually happen to him? He had no hope and wanted and desired nothing. he was brought into the safest of all safe places. Life in him was almost extinguished, but it was a good way of living, because there was almost nothing that hurt anymore. If he could just get this money, and if he could just get a novel written, the gods only knew about what, maybe several novels, then he would be off the hook. He wanted to get that novel written; it was a project he had had in mind for several years, but he couldn't get started, although he had sat down at his typewriter day after day and written a few lines, but he couldn't work it out. He was tired before he had begun. He had no faith in himself, and that was a prerequisite for being able to write the novel; for that reason he actually wanted to believe in himself, but he couldn't without having first written the novel. Things had closed in around him, he felt exhausted, he thought, but now at least he would get some money. He would have to use it wisely so it didn't run out right away, because then there would be no respite, and respite was what he needed.

He was the only person to get off at this station, as the train continued north to the coastal towns, and he cut across the dusty street in front of the station and went into the country store to ask for directions to Hiffs' house. He was given some preliminary information, and he could ask again when he got closer. He walked along the road with its thin grass and patches of heather and looked at the old-fashioned houses with towers or facades that were located closest to the station, but which soon gave way to log cabins and fake halftimbering or roofless, whitewashed concrete cubes. Soon he had left the more densely populated area, and the houses now lay scattered in the woods, each with its own path, its own boxes for milk bottles and mail.

At the eighth road on the right, he turned off and headed straight for the coast, for the wind now came straight toward him, and it smelled salty and fresh. A few hundred meters farther down the road, he ran into three lumberjacks eating lunch, and learned from them that he needed to take the first path on the left, then he would soon be there. As he walked down the path, he automatically felt his pocket to see if the paper was still there; it was, he wasn't nervous. Hiffs couldn't get out of paying him the ten thousand, because he had done what he had been asked to do.

The woods opened up a bit in front of him, and he noticed a grass-covered log cabin with two wings at the edge of the woods, which had to be Hiffs' house. The windows were open and the curtains were billowing, and when he came closer, he noticed that there was a meadow in front of the house and behind it some woods that must be very close to the sea. He didn't quite know how to make his entrance, whether to knock at the front door or go around the house to see if there were other doors or if Hiffs might be sitting outside, as one might expect on a day like this.

Tom followed the north wing of the house where there was a door that couldn't be the main entrance, and he stopped at the gable of the north wing and looked down over the meadow, where a couple of blackbirds were hopping around on large molehills, toward the last stretch of woods before the dunes, a maze of bushy trees with gnarled, tangled branches. He took a few more steps and saw Hiffs sitting with his eyes closed in a deck chair on the patio between the two wings. For a second, Tom thought of retreating; maybe he could walk around in the woods for a while or go down to the beach and let Hiffs finish his nap, but at that moment Hiffs opened his eyes and said, 'So, it's you, Tom. Well, how nice.' He got up from his chair and walked over to Tom.

'You sure got here in a hurry, Tom, and you look exhausted. Have you been working all night? Want some coffee?'

'Thanks,' Tom said, looking around the patio, where the grass was growing high between the paving blocks. 'Nice place you've got here.'

'Isn't it, though,' Hiffs said, nodding. 'This is my paradise. Have a seat and make yourself comfortable while I make the coffee.'

90

'Thanks,' Tom said, walking back and forth on the patio. So this was where Hiffs sat soaking up sun like some mystic from the Middle Ages, happy with life and sure of himself. He had understood it all, let things run their course. He had nothing undone to look back on. Everyone should be that lucky! Tom felt mistreated. Everything had gone right for Hiffs, and everything had gone wrong for himself, so that he hardly knew where he was and never counted on finding out. Could it be due to anything other than a basic injustice in life, which equipped people in different ways and let some of them mature happily while others were left to rot? Hiffs would probably claim that every individual had adequate possibilities, everyone was in control of his own life, but Tom didn't believe that; men served invisible powers who took them wherever they wanted to take them. Hiffs had been lucky, he had gotten into one of the right currents, Tom into one of the wrong ones. Although it might be his own fault and flaw that he was the way he was, it was nevertheless lack of energy that was the main cause, and that was not his fault. He had never been capable of asking himself the question of how to get more energy in such a way that he had any chance of getting it. The question arose only as a wish, which dissipated again in common, ordinary fatigue. He had always been tired; Hiffs didn't know that feeling.

Hiffs came out with a tray, which he put down on a light garden table that was next to his deck chair.

'Pull up a chair,' he said, crawling under the blanket in the deck chair.

Tom picked up an armchair and sat down by the table.

'You aren't doing anything?' he said dubiously to Hiffs.

Hiffs shook his head.

'Personally, I couldn't take it,' Tom said.

'I don't imagine you're doing too much yourself,' Hiffs said amicably, 'but I know what you mean. You want to create something. I don't. Have some coffee, Tom.'

Tom poured himself some coffee and took a piece of toast. 'Want to see what I've written?' Tom said, starting to hunt for the paper in his inside pocket.

'By all means, Tom,' Hiffs said.

'I got a few spots on the paper,' Tom said, 'but I thought you ought to have it the way it was.'

He handed the paper to Hiffs, and he could feel his heart thumping and his nerves tensing all over his body so that he felt renewed and able to do anything; his breathing was deep and slow, and a concentration he had never known before had settled in his eyes and behind his forehead so that he could register the slightest movement that might reveal Hiffs' opinion.

Hiffs unfolded the paper, and Tom saw how his eyes followed the lines, then he considered for a moment, read the lines again and thought some more, so that a cold fear spread inside Tom, now that he saw that there was no spontaneous yes, but that the matter had to be considered. He didn't understand what could be wrong; it seemed to him that the matter was clear, but Hiffs kept staring straight ahead with this inscrutable look that revealed nothing other than what anyone could guess, that Hiffs was considering the matter.

Suddenly Hiffs turned to Tom, and Tom already knew in advance what the words meant that followed.

'It's not worth a thing, Tom,' Hiffs said.

Tom felt himself falling from this place, but Hiffs' voice reached him.

'I can't give you the money, Tom,' Hiffs said.

'No,' Tom said, getting up, 'I guess you can't, so I'd better get going.'

'Sit down, Tom,' Hiffs said, 'there's no train for another hour.'

'I know,' Tom said. 'But I'll have to walk home anyway. You wouldn't happen to have some cigarettes?'

'Sure,' Hiffs said, getting up and returning a little later with a pack. 'Smoke to your heart's content.'

Tom tore the pack open.

'You're a charlatan, Hiffs,' Tom said. 'I suspect you're playing missionary. What is it you're educating me to become? Do you think by any chance I could have done a better job? What's wrong with it anyway? It *is* true, it *is* real, I couldn't go any deeper.'

'But you're not serious about it, Tom. And an honesty that doesn't mean anything to you, do you think that holds any meaning for me?'

Tom started to protest.

'No, Tom, for you this isn't serious. Your poem is written by a saurian, a demon, for whom even this last honesty is a matter of indifference. Reality is not indifferent, Tom, every individual must find a point of departure in despair and then grope his way out as best he can.'

'Is that what you did?' Tom said a bit sarcastically.

'You're not going to believe this. But maybe I did, Tom. Only I can't teach you how, because you're not capable of turning your own experiences into something exemplary and creating your own useful self.'

'I'm not even here,' Tom said to himself.

'I know, Tom, but then *get* here,' Hiffs said.

'It's too hard,' Tom mumbled, 'I can't. I'd have to be like you, I'd have to have energy, luck. But I can't, you know, I can't do it the way you can, I've never been able to, and it's not fair for you to sit there and plague me with your lofty phrases, which mean something to you but will never be of any use to me.'

'But I'm not doing a thing, you know,' Hiffs said. 'It won't hurt you to listen to what I have to say.'

'I'm afraid,' Tom said.

'It won't be long, Tom,' Hiffs said. 'Then you'll be wandering around again aimlessly, not knowing where you are. Why did you come out here so soon, why didn't you stay where you were, with your little reality, why didn't you let it calm you down, why didn't you say: Now I have tasted reality, now I shall never want to taste anything else; I am nothing, and I can do nothing, but if there is such a thing as reality, then let it come to me, and I shall welcome it and never make it larger or smaller but let it be whatever it is: sorrow and fear, bitterness and remorse. I shall make it my permanent guest and my secret, and it shall stay with me. It is my house, my abode.'

'Why did you call me,' Tom said, 'when you knew everything about me, why did you call me?'

'I wanted to see you one more time, Tom,' Hiffs said.

'Why didn't you leave me in peace?'

'But it doesn't mean anything, Tom,' Hiffs said. 'It doesn't hurt any more than before, and if it does hurt, then it'll soon pass, because there's nothing in you that is resolute, nothing that is constant. Nothing is as necessary as reality, Tom, and what life is all about is to create a habitat for what's real.'

'I don't have any money, you've got to lend me some money so I can get home, Hiffs.'

'No, Tom, I'm not giving you any money.'

'But you can't lure me all the way out here to your cursed, real place and let me walk home. You can't mean that, Hiffs, you couldn't be that cruel.'

Hiffs smiled.

'Hiffs!'

'No, Tom.'

'I know I should have bought a round-trip ticket, but I used some of the money because I had to have some cigarettes to help me get through the night. It was stupid of me, but I was so sure you would give me the money.'

'How could you be so sure, Tom?'

'I was as hard on myself as I could be.'

'That's a cliché, Tom. You told yourself that it sounded hard, but you didn't want to risk setting things up so that you would have to make a new beginning . . .'

'I don't *have* any energy, Hiffs.'

'No energy, Tom? Energy is waiting for you everywhere. Nobody has energy, energy is something you acquire.'

'Maybe you're right, Hiffs, but lend me ten kroner. I'm telling you, I have nothing, my wife has left me and taken the typewriter with her, I have no food, no kerosene to heat my house with.'

'I'm not giving you a thing, Tom.'

'Do you want me to leave, then?'

94

'Leave whenever you want to.'

Tom looked down at the paving; he was tired, he was less agitated now.

'Why are you calling me a demon, Hiffs?' he said.

'Because apparently you're here, and yet you're nowhere.'

Tom gave a dry laugh.

'I should have been a murderer, then I could have taken the money from you.'

'No one murders for money they don't want to do anything with.'

'No, Hiffs, you're right about everything you say. What do you think I ought to do, if I can do anything at all, because I don't know how to do anything, I've known that for a long time, for a very long time. Do you think I should commit suicide?'

'You did that a long time ago, Tom.'

'Then you won't send my wife the ten thousand, if I do it now for the second time?'

'No, Tom, I won't send your wife the ten thousand.'

'I had hoped you would.'

'But you don't care about your wife, Tom, now don't give me this sentimental bit.'

'No, Hiffs, but I do kind of, I didn't know that until yesterday, but I didn't dare write it down because I was afraid you'd laugh at me. But she does mean something to me, Hiffs, she's the only person who means anything to me in the whole world.'

'Then hurry back to her, Tom, hurry back to town and tell her what you've realized, get a permanent job, build your house, have children, and honor her faithfully until death do you part. Don't give her time to become bitter and settle down with someone else.'

'Lend me ten kroner, Hiffs.'

'No, Tom, but now you'd better leave; if you walk fast, you'll be back in town sometime tomorrow morning. Maybe a truck will pick you up, then you'll be there this afternoon or tonight.'

'My shoes are worn out, Hiffs.'

'Then you'll feel the road better, Tom.'

95

Tom stumbled to his feet.

'Have a good trip, Tom,' Hiffs said, raising his hand in a parting gesture.

Tom couldn't answer; he walked away with a lump in his throat from anger at having to walk seventy kilometers, and he knew there was no truck driver alive who would pick him up, because the guy would take one look at his clothes and his face, and then he wouldn't have a chance of getting a ride.

He stumbled over some tree roots after getting into the woods; he felt the earth hit him in the face and decided to stay there because it felt good to be lying still, not wanting to do anything. He thought about Etna, he wished she would come by and find him and raise his head and put a cool, wet cloth on his forehead and wash the blood off his nose and his lips, because he was bleeding. She ought to come and care for him a little, he thought, and comfort him and say a few kind words to him, for he needed kind words just now, but she was probably in bed with some salesman, because her needs were great, otherwise she wouldn't look so dissatisfied, but he couldn't, he couldn't, he was too small.

He raised his head a little and looked around, but he didn't feel like getting up, he just crawled forward on his stomach between the trees where the moss was thick like pillows, and there he remained and let the lethargy come, so that he hardly heard the sound of the wind in the tops of the fir trees or the screeching of the sea gulls from the beach or the blows of the ax and the drivers' encouraging calls to their nags. It would be all right for Hiffs to find him here, he thought, whenever he did think; he didn't care, he had the right to lie here, it wasn't for Hiffs to decide when he should go back to town. But when the afternoon turned cooler, he shivered and got up and walked around aimlessly in the woods, because he didn't want to go home, he didn't want to and he couldn't.

When the sun began to sink below the treetops, he sat down in the thicket right behind Hiffs' cottage, and after an hour had gone by, sure enough, he saw Hiffs walking down toward the beach with a couple of large tin boxes under his arms. He could have shouted with delight at his good fortune, and he had barely seen Hiffs disappear around the first bend in the path before he ventured out from his hiding place and walked around the north wing. Everything was still in its place; as he expected, Hiffs had sat there sunning himself all day long. The French doors leading into the house stood wide open, and he could walk right in.

He looked around the living room for a logical place, but there was no desk, just a few armchairs with linen covers, a couple of bookshelves along the walls with some books scattered in them, a table in front of the fireplace. He stuck his hands down behind the books, he searched through the papers under the table by the fireplace; then he walked into the room in the north wing where there was a bed, a chair, and a table. He tried under the pillow, opened the closet, and ransacked the pockets of the clothes, but he found only eighty-five øre in coins. He went out in the kitchen and checked all the cups, bowls, and platters, and then into the bathroom, where he shook the water glass, but all he could find was the eighty-five øre.

He shivered with despair when he stood on the patio again, and for a moment he thought of taking one of the chairs along and selling it in the railroad town, but it was hopeless, he couldn't sell anything without arousing suspicion. He suddenly started running down the path leading to the beach; a couple of magpies flew up screeching as he raced across the meadow. He saw the shadows of the enchanted forest whirling and retreating around him, and he almost couldn't get his breath, but he had to move on. Cutting through the dunes, he ran down across the beach and saw Hiffs some distance out on the sea with his sails to the offshore breezes, which came up after warm days like this.

Tom ran out on the wharf, and he yelled as loud as he could: 'I am impotent, Hiffs!' Exhausted and out of breath, he sighed and waited for Hiffs to turn his boat into the wind and head for the wharf and give him the ten thousand, for now there was nothing left to say. Now he was on the premises of reality, now they could laugh at him, but he had to have that money.

To his amazement he saw Hiffs continue out to sea, although he surely must have heard that he was being called, but maybe Hiffs was mulling over what he had said, or he couldn't turn his boat around just like that, he would have to tack up against the wind so as not to capsize. The sun had begun to set behind the woods, far out the light flowed flat over the sea, it was almost perfectly calm now that the wind had turned, and the water glistened like metal. Tom looked at it fearfully, for he saw that Hiffs was sailing farther and farther away, and when the sun had disappeared, the water shivered, and there was no mistaking the fact that night was on its way, the shadows had already gathered.

The night rose from the earth, and Tom sat hunched over all the way out on the bathing pier, afraid of everything that was happening so inevitably. If only Etna had been there next to him, at least he could have said a few words to her, so that he would know that he was alive when he heard her answer or her breath, and that he was not just a lump of fear in a darkness growing ever darker. Hiffs wasn't going to return, he knew that now, he had sailed away to other regions and had taken his money with him. He could go up and sleep in his house, but he didn't dare, for the walls would whisper with Hiffs' voice and repeat and repeat what Hiffs had said, that he was a demon who didn't exist. It was true, it was true, Tom thought, he didn't exist, he was nothing but fear as he had always been, and everything that went into him went on to fear and became nothing, and everything that came out of him had first passed the courts and streets of fear and had the withering faces of death. He couldn't give, he couldn't take; it all belonged to fear.

If only he could let go now, if only he could be carried off to a state of unconsciousness now, then he wouldn't complain, even if he fell asleep and slipped into the water, because he would not venture out in it himself, it was cold and cruel, one shouldn't demand the impossible of a demon of the legion of fear; and all those cells and fibers that were physically his, after all, they could only tire, they could decide nothing, they obeyed only the

Mighty Being who had forced his way into him and taken possession of him many, many years ago.

And he suddenly remembered his childhood with its vast lawns, its enclosures between hedges, and the hours that echoed ten-thousandfold; he remembered the quiet attics, the fragrant rooms, and days that rose from his consciousness like a tingling in his heart; he remembered his first truly happy thoughts and his dreams as they traveled down safe streams of nerves. But one day fear had arrived, and there had been nothing he could do. There had been no road back to this reality, which was now sucked out and dried up and could not be brought back to life during a single lifetime. He needed a thousand lives.

He ought to struggle for reality, but he couldn't struggle, because his fear was *so* strong. Even his novel would never get written, because his reality consisted of three words; that was no novel, it was merely a miserable little truth that ruled his life.

Night had surrounded him, and when he had gotten used to the great darkness, he crawled up laboriously and walked in on the beach. He looked at the masses of dunes that glistened dimly and at the forest whose glow had now vanished, and he turned around and looked out over the ocean, where Hiffs must be sailing somewhere on his way toward a reality which he, Tom, would never understand in the next ten thousand years. He was, after all, at the saurian stage; his blood was cold with fear, and that was something he would never conquer.

But he picked up a large round pebble and threw it out in the water; when he heard the plop, he exclaimed: 'I am here!' Then he retreated and walked in across the dunes and down the forest path, and he felt he was getting used to seeing where he was and where he walked. He passed Hiffs' house on the run so that he wouldn't be pursued by what might still be lurking in there, and he didn't stop until he was past the first street lights in the railroad town. In front of the hotel, a couple of large refrigerated vans were parked. He had better go in and have a beer and make friends with the drivers.

Niels Ingwersen

Afterword

A few books achieve cult status, and *The Impostor* is one of them.
When the novel appeared in 1957, it immediately attracted the
attention of young intellectuals, a group in society that always
tends to be searching for the book that will capture, illuminate,
or expose their experience of reality. *The Catcher in the Rye* and
Catch 22 are just two American examples that readily come to
mind, and both suggest that works that gain such status not only
proffer sympathy for the hero or anti-hero, but also demon-
strate a keen sense of the problematic in the natures of their
protagonists.

Many cult books soon lose their admirers, but Danes – like
many others – continue to be fascinated with *The Impostor*, just
as Americans still find pleasure in, or get riled by, reading J. D.
Salinger or Joseph Heller.

Why would this Peter Seeberg novel, his second, have that
appeal? It has neither the vernacular charm of Holden Caul-
field's wry and sad commentary nor Heller's/Yossarian's gro-
tesque, anarchistic humor. In fact, *The Impostor* may seem to
offer the reader only slim pickings, and the English-speaking
reader ought to know that the title of the novel in Danish, *Fugls
føde*, literally and inelegantly should be translated as 'bird's
feed.' When looking up the expression 'fugls føde' in an adequate Danish dictionary, one is informed that it is used to de-
scribe meagerness; it is thus hardly an expression with positive
connotations. And, as will become clear, Seeberg, like Salinger
and Heller, directs a stinging indictment against his culture.

The plot seems meager indeed and scarcely appealing: its main character is a shifty, lazy fellow, a bit of a writer, but not a man who would ever take a permanent job to support himself and his wife, Etna. This marginal man, whose name is Tom (the word means 'empty' in Danish), is offered a chance to earn a pretty penny by a well-to-do acquaintance, Hiffs, if he writes something that is real. Tom tries, and his inner trials and tribulations, as he is forced to be what he detests, i.e., mentally active, occupy a good deal of the narrative. Eventually, he presents the results – a slim confession that is intended to capture the essence of his meager existence or non-existence:

> My eyes are blind,
> my hands are withered,
> my soul is afflicted with annihilation [p.76].

He is quite satisfied with his 'little poem,' which he entitles 'My Reality'; and in order to impress Hiffs with his scrupulous honesty, he exposes his wretchedness by adding 'I'm writing this to earn ten thousand' (p.77).

Hiffs, however, rejects that poetic result as lacking in reality for Tom, refuses to pay the exasperated Tom the money, and leaves – he sails his boat into the darkness of the evening. He does not seem to hear how Tom, in a last attempt to earn the money, adds one line to his 'poem' to try to make it real: 'I am impotent' (p.97). The narrative ends as Tom plans to catch a ride back to town, where he hopes to track down, and become reconciled with, his wife.

The plot hardly offers flashy action or characters, but it should be noted that Seeberg has cut out a distinguished career for himself by focusing on aspects of reality often ignored by writers of fiction. Such a perspective was already apparent in his first novel, *Bipersonerne* ('Minor Characters,' 1956), which in a sense gave the direction for Seeberg's entire oeuvre. The novel is set in Berlin during the Second World War, but Seeberg typically focuses on characters that never take center stage historically. Such peripheral characters are featured prominently in much of Seeberg's fiction, and readers are thus faced with people who, in a sense, are given a paradoxical role. On the one hand, they are people who are out of touch with reality but attempting, vainly, to reach reality – that common theme in Western literature; on the other hand, though peripheral, they are people whose experiences Seeberg implicitly insists are significant. Seeberg consequently offers such people center stage and casts a less than flattering light on those players who are traditionally seen as the major ones. He is a subtle humorist who takes delight in unmasking pretentiousness, hollow rhetoric, and fraudulent emotionalism and intellectualism.

Seeberg occupies a special position in Danish letters. In some sense he may be compared to Villy Sørensen (another author published in this series). Both aim high in the demands they place upon their readers; both command much respect among such readers – and both are incisive, humorous, and relentless critics of their culture.

A few facts about Peter Seeberg (b. 1925) should suggest that, like Sørensen, he is an unabashed intellectual engaged in judging his time. He earned a degree in comparative literature but has worked for years as the director of a Danish regional museum (which also has entailed his participation in archeological explorations and excavations as well as his publishing in that field). The early articles he published while still a student, on Nietzsche and Wittgenstein, indicate his fascination with philosophers who have discussed the limitations of language. That concern became a major issue within the artistic movement that has broadly been called Modernism and, even later, within one dominant critical response to Modernism labeled Deconstruction.

As of now Seeberg has published five novels, three collections of short stories, two plays, two manuscripts for movies or television, and some nonfiction that appeared in limited, privately published books or pamphlets. Several of his works have been translated into other languages, including *The Impostor*. On the surface Seeberg's novels seem fairly realistic, although readers will notice, as they do in *The Impostor*, that Seeberg's keen sense of the minutiae of very ordinary life is juxtaposed with a modernistic allegoric-symbolic kind of discourse that forces them to interpret the text.

That technique is clearly used in *The Impostor*: in spite of himself, Tom is by necessity involved with many details of mundane reality; thus, the reader encounters something akin to a psychological realism, but elements in the text simultaneously give the impression of abstraction, for the setting cannot be localized geographically, and the names of the protagonists, such as Tom, Hiffs, and Etna, point to no specific culture.

It has been suggested that Seeberg's works gradually became more and more humorous.[1] Especially some of his short stories give convincing evidence for that claim, but it should be noted that Seeberg's technique, tooled to expose grim and stark truths about human beings, bears a strong resemblance to the merriment that one encounters in Samuel Beckett's bleak, absurd, and hilarious indictments of modern culture.

It might well be that it was such criticism that hit home when *The Impostor* was first published. With that novel Seeberg created a protagonist that seemed to be the very embodiment of the modern 'hollow man.'[2] In addition, Seeberg makes it quite clear that his book was intended not only to capture modern social and existential reality, but to put it into focus by contrasting it with the past. Seeberg does so through his settings, which are, as mentioned, made somewhat abstract so they assume that allegoric-symbolic function. In fact, the working title of the novel was 'Places' – and as Tom travels, he moves through various locations that belong to different cultural periods.[3] As he heads for the city to meet Hiffs, he leaves his no-man's-land, quite representative of his existence, in the border region between the country and suburbia, moves through modern wastelands, and arrives in the cityscape of the nineteenth century. Seeberg may not be a modernist in the sense of a James Joyce or Djuna Barnes or the authors of the so-called French new novel of the 1950s, but his technique pointedly calls attention to the elements of the narrative that the reader is called upon to interpret.

That approach appealed to a generation that had grown accustomed to being – in fact was expected to be – drawn into the creative process in order to confront themselves. Modernism has always refused the reader that self-satisfaction or self-righteousness which was the reader's reward in the nineteenth-century bourgeois *Bildungsroman*: I have become a wise and well-integrated prominent member of society. Modernist readers, on the contrary, are denied that sense of having reached a final, satisfactory station in life, and with Seeberg's novel those readers seemed ready to see themselves in Tom, a man with a 'minimal consciousness' (p.20). Tom, rightly or not, was very likely accepted as a common denominator by those intellectuals who observed themselves with a solid portion of self-loathing. Readers of such writers as Sartre and Camus, as well as other contemporaries, were quick to recognize a hollow man.

At certain times, when intellectuals find a cause of a pragmatic cut, as they did in the late 1960s and early 1970s, their urge for self-chastisement is minimized or redirected, and during such periods Modernism is often shunned as being elitist. Seeberg was subjected to some severe criticism from the New Left generation of 1968. There can, however, be little doubt that present day 'yuppie'-intellectuals are once again being drawn to works that scrutinize and chastise the culture they have helped shape. The appeal of – or fascination with – *The Impostor* may at times subside, but its 'abstractness' will enable the novel to transcend a given period of time and cause readers to see themselves in the text.

This critique of intellectuals or pseudo-intellectuals was quite common in the 1950s and can be found in the works of a number of authors who questioned the wisdom and integrity of the 'educated' person, the product of traditional *Bildung*. Many authors of that decade seemed to echo Martin A. Hansen's and H. C. Branner's exposures of confused and untruthful intellectuals, for the former's *Løgneren* (1950, *The Liar*, 1954) and the latter's *Rytteren* (1949, *The Riding Master*, 1951) had a tremendous impact on young writers. Some works in the same critical vein, but less derivative, attracted a good deal of attention and were, for a time, discussed widely. Most prominent were Tage Skou-Hansen's *De nøgne træer* (1957, *The Naked Trees*, 1957), Aksel Heltoft's *Chefen* (1958, 'The Boss'), Poul Ørum's *Skyggen ved din højre hånd* (1959, 'The Shadow by Your Right Hand'), and Poul Vad's *De nøjsomme* (1960, 'Modest People'). It should be noted, however, that these texts, with the possible exception of Skou-Hansen's, if not gathering dust, are hardly fascinating modern readers. So why is *The Impostor* so alive today?

Very likely, Seeberg's criticism cuts much deeper than proposed above, and his analytical probe of Tom tends to go further than to a self-righteous exposure of that character's weaknesses.

What grants relief even to readers who savor literary self-flagellation is the presence in *The Impostor* of Hiffs, who obviously seems to be presented as an alternative to Tom. Hiffs is humorous, relaxed, perceptive, and alert. In addition, he is rich, smart, charming, attractive, and apparently in complete control of his life. He takes delight in the world that surrounds him, and – to add another of his impressive credentials – he has made the noble choice of leaving material culture behind for an enjoyment of nature and art. From his words, Hiffs emerges as one of those cultural heroes of Western civilization who seems to have all the right values and attitudes. It may seem quite just that it is this well-adjusted, wise figure who passes judgment on Tom. He embodies the ultimate intellectual dream of power – maybe a subtle, spiritual power, but a power to be reckoned with – as Tom, humbled and humiliated, must recognize.

Thus, the reader seems to encounter a clear-cut contrast, but that contrast is subtly undercut in many ways by the text. That discovery may take several readings to make, but when first made, the balance between the two figures remains disturbed and the supposed contrast between them becomes highly complicated and problematic.

First of all, the reader – in particular those who are aware of the implications of the original Danish title, i.e., 'bird's feed' – may recall that what a bird eats on any given day is several times its own weight; thus, the 'pickins' may not be so slim after all. Tom certainly resents doing anything that requires an effort, but as he scurries through his daily life, he is really very active – trying to get 'free' cigarettes, sardines, bus rides, or whatever. Furthermore, the English title of the book, *The Impostor*, eventually comes to ring quite true, for the readers may begin to see an impostor in Hiffs, too.

Elucidation is needed.

It is necessary, once again, to go back to the working title of the novel, 'Places.' When Hiffs and Tom meet, it is in the old-fashioned part of the city, and when they later strike their bargain in a restaurant of Hiffs' choice, that scene also harkens back to the past. As they talk, Tom soon grows tired of Hiffs' abstract musings over the necessity of values, and he accuses him of being preoccupied with outdated problems and suggests that Hiffs' thinking is a symptom of a personal crisis:

'Frankly, I think you've started taking things much too seriously,' Tom said. 'What's all that claptrap you went on about really supposed to mean? I mean, I already know all that garbage; it's the same old stuff, as you well know. What's the point? You aren't by any chance going through some kind of personal crisis? Because I sure don't see what you want with me today' [p.43].

The last question is well taken. When Hiffs first asks Tom to write something that is real, he may seem like a benevolent rescuer or redeemer who is attempting to save Tom from himself, but immediately after Tom's question Hiffs poses his offer. In light of Tom's assessment of Hiffs' situation, it can be suggested that Hiffs is asking Tom to write something that is real because he realizes that Tom has a better grasp of reality than he does himself. In fact, the offer can be seen as a veiled cry for help on the part of a man of traditional culture to the modern human being, seemingly a person who has cut his ties with the past, for Hiffs has understood that the values of his old-fashioned culture can no longer sustain him.[4]

It is Hiffs who is asking to be rescued by someone who possesses the ability to survive within the modern chaos that he himself fears.

That reading of *The Impostor* may seem farfetched – and the contours drawn here maybe a bit sharp – but, once it comes to mind, it becomes difficult to exorcize it, and in that lies the peculiar fascination and strength of Seeberg's narrative. Not only does the novel expose a shabby nowhere man in a way that is far from unusual, but it also reveals the cultural hero to be, maybe first and foremost, a fraud, a weak impostor who quite vampirically attempts to gain the help of the survivor. It is quite easy to loathe Tom and to be seduced into admiring Hiffs, only to be awakened into shocked awareness by Seeberg.

It would be naive to maintain that a complete reversal has taken place, for everything negative said about Tom still stands, but Hiffs emerges as a figure who has even less contact with reality than Tom has. 'A neat couple,' as the Danish critic Henning Mortensen calls them,[5] but it should be noted that whereas Tom manages to exist quite well within his nihilism, Hiffs cannot stand to live in a world with no sustaining values.

If the above is a description of the real situation, one can easily understand why Hiffs must reject Tom's 'poem.' First, Hiffs is right on target when he points out that the wretched mood of Tom's lines is unimportant to the author; Tom may sound paralyzed and suicidal, but, as mentioned, he actually manages his petty existence quite competently. Second, and more importantly, the statement may capture in a devastating manner Hiffs' existential crisis, and thus Hiffs, who hoped that Tom would provide him with a renewed relationship to reality, now sees his hopes dashed.

As Hiffs sails away from the land and into the darkness (death?), Tom throws a stone in the water and, so to speak, completes his 'poem.' Without any thought of monetary gain or of Hiffs – who was continually on his mind as he wrote – he states, 'I am here' (p.99), and he prepares to continue his life much as it was before. That line, however, could hardly be said by or about Hiffs.

It should finally be observed that Tom is a bit of an artist. He dreams of writing a novel that will expose all hypocrisy (*The Impostor* fulfills a good deal of that promise), and Hiffs initially appears much like the old-fashioned patron, that benefactor (also economically) of the artist, but behind the mask of this benevolent patron exists his fear of an emerging world with which he cannot cope. Audiences, like patrons, have always wanted artists to perform to their liking and have wanted artists to provide order when chaos was threatening. Artists were those who had to give answers to the disturbing questions about existence.

Tom, citizen of modernity, refuses – without knowing it or wanting it – to play the artist's time-honored role and thus denies the patron and audience what they need and traditionally expect from art. It is fair to say that *The Impostor* does the very same thing to its expectant audience, thus becoming an understandably disturbing book that is not easily forgotten.

One reason for the novel's appeal may also be that Seeberg, in his personal fashion, foreshadowed – and wrote in keeping with – that recent, powerful movement within Western philosophy/criticism called Deconstruction. After having delivered his blows at Tom, Seeberg starts – much like Kierkegaard in his treatment of his ethical person – undercutting and undermining the figure who seems to be the epitome of what is good and right. Deconstruction is often equated with nihilism, and *The Impostor* may seem to leave readers with very little on which they can rest their hopes. For unlike Kierkegaard, Seeberg does not postulate a new consciousness that was intended to save the individual from *angst*, but neither does he cave in to a facile, defeatist nihilism. If the text is nihilistic, it is so in the sense that a rejection of past values and ideals has been deemed necessary in order to wipe the slate clean. Tom may make a well-taken point – whether one agrees with him or not – when he calls past culture garbage, for apparently only he who refuses to be seduced by the past has the (unconscious) power to survive. This is a bleak vision – once again, Beckett comes to mind – but it seems that only through a rejection of outdated cultural values can human beings say, as Tom finally does, 'I am here.'

The same, in fact, can be said about several of Beckett's main characters: they may be alienated, seem hapless, and have little chance of ever escaping their miserable existences – the waiting for Godot will continue, and Winnie will never get away from her sandheap (*Happy Days*, 1961) – but they are not defeated human beings. Beckett's trapped people and Tom, whose chance or will to change his life is minimal, may also remind readers of the protagonist in Ivan Goncharov's *Oblomov* (1859). In spite of Oblomov's grand plans and his prodding by others, his life dwindles away, but it would nevertheless be wrong to call him a defeated person, for spending a life in total passivity and oblivion is his own decision. There is a significant difference between Oblomov and Ivan Turgenev's tired, superfluous, and defeated men, who left their mark so strongly on Western literature during the latter third of the nineteenth century. One can easily speak of a Turgenev tradition, but hardly of a Goncharov tradition; nevertheless, both Beckett and Seeberg suggest that, in spite of the way Oblomov's life turned out, they recognize that he 'is here.'

Tom is an appalling character; Seeberg emphasizes that, but, as he implies, Hiffs is worse. Through that implication Seeberg joins rank with Kierkegaard and Nietzsche in a radical contempt of their respective cultures' ideal figures.

Deconstruction makes language suspect, and in *The Impostor* Tom acts toward Hiffs like the deconstructive critic, but when Tom tries to produce something that he assumes will be attuned to Hiffs' wavelength, he gets his just desserts. When Hiffs rejects Tom's 'poem,' he deconstructs not only Tom's hypocritical effort, but also the language that Hiffs himself, and those like him, have used to depict what in reality has been a spiritual bankruptcy – and this irony is at the core of good, witty deconstructionist criticism.

It may seem that the term Deconstruction has been used in an unfettered manner in the last few pages; there, it has been suggested that Kierkegaard and Nietzsche might be considered deconstructive critics; furthermore, no one had yet even uttered the term Deconstruction when Seeberg wrote his novel. Deconstruction, however, can be considered to be (and many might disagree with the following) not a fad of the late twentieth century that soon may fade – fashions in literary criticism are about as short-lived as those in clothing – but an impulse, a quality of language, one that is age-old and that storytellers and writers, especially when at odds with their times, are compelled to invoke for the sake of a scathing and necessary undermining of the cultural 'reign.'

In conclusion, to engage in that time-honored deconstructive activity is hardly nihilistic – even if the creations of such a severely antagonistic imagination produce a type like Tom, for he ironically offers more hope for the future than the fading idol Hiffs can. Devastating criticism of the past, as that past exists in – and tries to take control of – the present, is needed, especially because language must be liberated from leveling, manipulative usage that robs it of meaning.

By being mercilessly deconstructive, Seeberg manages to make his disclosure rewarding, for his story and diction, with their total lack of respect for any cultural icons, may result in a new critical awareness on the part of the reader – an awareness that surpasses Tom's listless existence and takes its point of departure in his final and honest statement: 'I am here.' Seeberg is too wise to posit any new cultural ideal, but his diction suggests that language which regains its meaning opens doors to reality. Here Seeberg may be echoing Wittgenstein and, so to speak, opposing the nihilistic deconstructionist, for it seems that the text called *The Impostor* proves that it is possible to fulfill the dream that Tom entertains – and very likely will never realize – that it is possible to write something that is 'pure, unadulterated exposure' (p.15).[6]

1   See Karen Syberg on Seeberg in Vol. VIII of *Dansk litteraturhistorie* (Copenhagen: Gyldendal, 1985), p.316.

2   T. S. Eliot's works were a major inspiration to the post-Second World War generation. These writers' attempt to capture their acute sense of crisis seems to be echoed in Hiffs' way of talking and in the language of 'the poem' that Tom makes up to please Hiffs.

3   See Hanne Marie Svendsen, *Romanens veje. Værkstedssamtaler med danske forfattere* (Copenhagen: Rasmus Fischers Forlag, 1966). Seeberg stresses that he differs from the French modernists in the sense that they focus only on the present, whereas he operates with 'all categories of time' (p.81). In addition, Seeberg discusses the genesis of the novel (p.84).

4   As early as 1963, Søren Baggesen suggested that Hiffs should not be taken at face value, but be recognized to be 'just as weak and impotent as Tom.' See Baggesen, 'Omstændelig omhu,' *Vindrosen*, 5 (1963), p.421. In my own article 'Nihilismen som livsgrundlag. En studie i Peter Seebergs *Fugls Føde*,' *Edda*, 68 (1968): 380-93, I have given a more detailed analysis of the reasons for viewing Hiffs negatively.

5   Henning Mortensen, 'Tomgang i en minusverden,' in *Mytesyn*, ed. Iben Holk (Copenhagen: Centrum, 1985), p.33.

6   The rendition of the Danish phrase 'uden præk, ren erkendelse' is fine, but the translator is up against formidable problems with 'præk' and even more so with 'erkendelse' – a word that tends to haunt Danish literature. An awkward translation of the above phrase is 'devoid of preaching and pure perception,' but it will readily be conceded that 'perception' does not capture the sense of 'erkendelse,' i.e., of the probing into the world that leads to a deeper existential understanding of the human lot (please pardon me for sounding like Hiffs!).

REFERENCES

Baggesen, Søren. 'Dansk prosamodernisme' in *Modernismen i dansk litteratur.* Ed. Jørn Vosmar. Copenhagen: Fremad, 1967. Pp.119-91.

———. 'Omstændelig omhu. Til belysning af virkelighedsorienteringen i Peter Seebergs forfatterskab.' *Vindrosen*, 5 (1963): 416-23.

Bondebjerg, Ib. *Peter Seeberg. En ideologikritisk analyse.* Grenå: GMT, 1972.

Brandt, Jørgen Gustava. 'Jeg'et og ingenmandsland.' In *Præsentation - 40 Danske Digtere efter Krigen.* Copenhagen: Gyldendal, 1963. Pp.137-40

Bredsdorff, Thomas. *Sære fortællere. Hovedtræk af ny dansk prosakunst.* Copenhagen: Gyldendal, 1967.

Brostrøm, Torben. 'Intellektets tankespærringer.' In *Dansk Litteratur Historie*, VI. Copenhagen: Politikens forlag, 1978. Pp.109-15.

Henneberg, Jens. 'Den eftertragtede indsigt.' *Exil*, 1 (1966): 89-91.

Holk, Iben, ed. *Mytesyn. En bog om Peter Seebergs forfatterskab.* Copenhagen: Centrum, 1985.

Ingwersen, Niels. 'Nihilismen som livsgrundlag. En studie i Peter Seebergs *Fugls føde*.' *Edda*, 68 (1967): 380-93.

Larsen, Finn Stein. 'Flodseng og kramkiste.' In *Mytesyn*. Pp.9-17.

Mandøe, Niels. 'Temaet i Peter Seeberg's *Fugls føde*.' *Dansk Udsyn*, 47 (1967): Pp.338-58.

Mortensen, Henning. 'Tomgang i en minusverden.' In *Mytesyn*. Pp.29-42.

Nissen, Jan. '*Fugls føde*. Peter Seebergs digtning.' *Kritik*, 2 (1968): 5-20.

Sandstrøm, Bjarne. 'Vejen mod havet. Om bevidstheden som problem i Peter Seebergs forfatterskab.' *Kritik*, 12 (1978): 39-64.

Sandstrøm, Bjarne. 'At forstå sine egne forudsætninger.' In *Danske digtere i det 20. århundrede*, IV. Ed. Torben Brostrøm & Mette Winge. Copenhagen: Gad, 1982. Pp.11-28.

Svendsen, Hanne Marie. *Romanens veje. Værkstedssamtaler med danske forfattere*. Copenhagen: Rasmus Fischers forlag, 1966. Pp.73-89.

Syberg, Karen. *Dansk litteraturhistorie*, VIII. Copenhagen: Gyldendal, 1985. Pp.311-16.

Thule, Vagn. *Peter Seeberg*. Copenhagen: Munksgaard, 1972.

Other volumes in the series
Modern Scandinavian Literature
in Translation include: